A GLANCE
AWAY

Also by **John Edgar Wideman**
and published by **Allison & Busby**

Damballah

Hiding Place

Sent for You Yesterday

Brothers and Keepers

A GLANCE AWAY

by John Edgar Wideman

Allison & Busby
London

This cased edition first published in 1986
by Allison & Busby Ltd
6a Noel Street, London W1V 3RB

Copyright © 1967 by John Edgar Wideman

British Library Cataloguing in Publication Data
Wideman, John Edgar
  A glance away.
  I. Title
  813'.54[F]   PS3573.I26
  ISBN 0-85031-739-8

Printed and bound in Great Britain by
Billings & Sons Ltd., Hylton Road, Worcester

To Homes
and the people who have made mine

PROLOGUE

It is afterall a way of beginning. To have never quite enough so hunger grows faster than appetites and satisfaction never comes.

On an April day insouciant after the fashion of spring insouciance the warm secret of life was shared with another. Bawling milk hungry mammal dropped in pain from flanks of a she. Him.

Fine, healthy boy, eight pounds seven ounces.

Mystery repeats itself to boredom. And he shall be called Eugene. In the name of the grandfather who balding, high on dago red, waited news in a cloud of garbage smelling smoke at the foot of steep, ringing marble stairs of Allegheny General Hospital.

—Wonder what they's doin' to my littlebaby. Martha better be all right. Freeda, I got me a grandson. Big 'un he's gonna be. Big and bad like his granddaddy Eugene. A big, bad nigger-Gene, said the tall baldpate man clomping on bunioned feet loudly up the stairs, shrugging off tentative back holding hands and small voice excited of pale receptionist starched white at desk. A bigniggerGene.

—You can't go up there sir.

—My little girl's up there lady. You hear me, my little Martha's there and nobody on God's green earth's gonna keep me from my girl. Off shuffling to tune of *Gimme that wine spudie-udie* he went, dedecorumed in glee of life renewed bearing his name, his flesh and blood redone forever in two bodies precious together under hospital blankets.

That man is crazy. Lord knows how much gut rotting wine he's drunk already today. Freeda's face, handsomely molded, skin lined finely under eyes and across her forehead testifying to three children grown and two dead seemed fixed in an attitude of fear and pride. Broad husband's back and long legs like cords in baggy trousers as they disappeared around a landing were for her so familiar that each time she found herself watching him leave a strange panic danced in her bowels. Girlish flutter of first romance, him insubstantial because he was so closely interwoven with her dreams. More hope than dream, hope that absence assaulted, changed to helplessness before a truth she fought not to conceive. Each time he would never come back. Rakish broad-brimmed hat, flapping trousers, the boy's swagger, his broad back swaying . . .

Up the forbidden stairs. Her Gene, and what did he fear. A curse dropped echoing in the high-walled foyer. He'll go there, and no one will stop him. He'll do it if it kills him.

Unguardedly the forbidden word dropped. Gene gone. It would never happen, could never happen to him, bold swiller of wine whose veins received it like sun. DaddyGene paperhanger, half-dago giant who handled his tools fine Italian handwise like short, dark men he worked beside. Hang that shit like two men. Later slouched in easy chair dangling over armrests, huge feet stretched to middle of livingroom, a king. Like when loaded, stumbling into kitchen, opening iceboxdoor and placing chair close to its exposed innards spoon in hand devouring every edible morsel and some that weren't.

How could he go away after all these years. But certainly I have learned, I am an old woman, children grown and dead, not much time for either of us. But please God, me first. Take me first if we can't go together.

She had spoken to her daughter in the kitchen. Martha, you must be patient. Clarence is young, headstrong. It's hard for him too. He hasn't done so badly up to now. With the way most of these young fellows act today, your Clarence ain't been half bad.

4

—But Mama, leaving me like this. If I ever needed him, it's now. Now when I'm carrying his baby. Just going off like he did. One minute standing talking to me in the bedroom, asking how I felt, how long the doctor thought it would be, if I needed anything—acting so gentle, so loving, as if he really cared. Talking the way he used to, before . . .

—He's young, Martha. Like you're young. He has to fight for a while, show himself now that he's found out what living with a woman really means that he can still love you. It has to be a different kind of love, cause after a month or a year the old kind gives out. It hurts, it scares them worse than it ever does us. He's young, hotblooded. No patience—everything has to come at once. Quick, easy, black and white with no waiting around. Right now I believe he just don't know how to wait, how to believe, how to hope. So you have to wait. Be there always when he comes back. And he will honey, he will. The man, and he's gonna be a man, loves you.

GENE, GENE THE PIPER'S SON STOLE A PIG AND AWAY HE RUN.

Belch innard deep lurched up through chest tasting garlic and stale wine, swaying, perched in throat, a honeyed song that danced smiling unto the old man's features. Of all the damndest things me drunk on these stairs upgoing to little skinny Martha, firstborn of my brood to see firstborn of her still secret brood somewhere hidden in loins of dark boy who came and courted and caught little Martha skinny's fancy, how drunk I am on that first drink neverending after paper is hung on walls with care and we don't care folding ladders, gathering tools cramped in pickup truck how many together we take and then home to Freeda still fine and fair whose skinny daughter lies as she did how many years ago the first time pale and long hair plaited over pillow, afraid, squeezing till blood stopped in my hand laid on her blue flowered shoulder she wept and was afraid as Martha dark eyes damp waits me winding up these white man's stairs and through silent corridors to her side.

OVER THE HILLS AND EVERYWHERE.

Please God let Clarence come. I need him now beside me. The pain, the pain God. For him, this flesh that is his, God, my husband's flesh. Clary, please come. Her eyes fixed on rectangular opening in the wall, dim edges visible around curtain serving as a door where if he would come, he must enter. Through gauzy space of curtain her eyes strained to catch any movement. Invisibly it fretted. Shifting outlines like hands moved behind it, becoming fuzzy, indistinct, absorbed by the whiteness of the walls, disappearing as if the walls melted and grew together under her intense stare. I want him so much. And nothing, no one answered because she was but a woman in pain, lone woman in hospital gown languid on her bed of pain. Clarence please come. The flimsy curtain danced. Only tears came that squinted through made a mist between her eyes and small wound in the white wall. She remembered how she had only a glimpse of the baby's red, wrinkled body, and then he was whisked away. Hygienic, uncontaminated by her closeness and need.

—I'm comin' girl. Little Martha yore Daddy's comin'. Don't let 'em take the little nigger away till I get there. His besotted voice quavering and resonant in echo chamber of marble halls reached her. Things had begun again. The dream of her pain so certain and complete had ended. Soon DaddyGene would fill the room with eagerness and brash, assuming ministrations. Authority of his movements, sour smell of wine as he leaned giddily rough cheek against her flesh to rub and kiss and whisper as he had always done to mend her bruised knees and feelings, treating his girl child as if nothing in the world could not be hugged away or forgotten in gentle rhythm of *Froggy went a courtin'* hummed while she bobbed like a cork on his slowly bouncing knee.

—Daddy—where is he Daddy?

—Ain't they told you where they took the little nigger. It ain't right snatching a woman's son afore she even gets to look at it good. You'd think it belonged to 'em, and you doing all the suffrin'. Just be still li'l Martha, I'll get 'em back in a minute. He's a big red 'un I bet. Bald just like his DaddyGene. I'm gonna see for myself, and bellowing, Nurse git in here with this child's baby, he stood up tall, still cock-hatted, face drawn into a parody of stern command and fierceness.

—That don't do any good, Daddy. It's supposed to be this way. There's germs in here.

—Well they's your germs, and I ain't got none you ain't got. We's all one family, and he might as well start gettin' used to us. Hey—bring that boy back here.

—Please Daddy, they'll come and chase you away. Please be still . . . just sit here next to me.

—Stop your crying li'l Martha. It's all over now girl. You're a woman ain't you. I know it's hard, I been through it many times, sittin' beside your mother, holdin' her hand while she cried and prayed. She even asked the Lord to kill 'er once, begged him just to let it all be over with. But she's a good woman, your mother is, girl, and I know you'll be just like 'er. So hush, it's all over now. You's safe and the young 'un probably sleepin' somewhere, dreamin' about his Mama. Hush li'l Martha, your hands is cold.

Bed dipped, receiving his whole weight as he unstraddled its edge lifting both feet to stretch out atop the blue spread.

—You know somethin', your Daddy don't feel too well. He's kinda sleepy, been workin' since early this morning, and I ain't as young as I used to be. The humming of *Froggy* grew less and less distinct shading off into deep wheezing sound of sudden, heavy sleep, song to snore that rumbled uneven and loud beside her. She looked at huge hand wrapped around, hiding hers, veins blue and intricate were raised thickly, seeming to strain against the skin which had begun to dry and grow thinner, gaining the waxlike quality common to children and old men. She thought of trees, fall, winter trees, branches spreading into delicate fan-shaped designs stark, naked in gray-yellow light. Nights filled with formless fears, with shapes that fed on darkness and grew at an incredible rate into threatening beasts, of her Daddy beside her, her body cached deep in a peaceful valley between warmth and bulk of her parents' sleeping flesh. *Now I lay me down to sleep.* How she had finally parted from Clarence that first night, exhausted, drained, awakening later to feel his naked back against hers and the sudden fear of finding only space in front of her eyes as morning filtered behind her through a thin paper blind into their borrowed room. Quickly, as if pursued she had turned away from the emptiness and drawn closer to his body, encircling him with her arms till he turned drowsy eyed and wrapped her into his.

—Clary, I think we're going to have a baby.

Guarded, unfamiliar words between mother and daughter. Alone together in kitchen; cooking sounds mellow, subdued as food simmered to a precise warmth and consistency just before serving time. Respite when Freeda's voice would come from far off, disembodied, trying to accustom herself to the girl who must suddenly share women's secrets. Uneasiness, even embarrassment as her advice had to take the form of intimacies revealed, experiences related that she was forced to recognize as her own and now her daughter's inheritance. So small and frail. Had she been like that? Barely developed, her little girl's body soon burdened with the weight of another life. Of two lives. Lean, dark stranger who it seemed only yesterday she had seen carting groceries at the big supermarket in a makeshift wagon propelled by baby carriage wheels. Man-boy three times a week sitting on front porch steps, lingering over good-night always until Martha told a second time her father wanted her to come to bed. The Lawson boy. Rather wild, but no worse than the rest, anxious to please, very polite and respectful in face of his elders—nice enough—wants to go to college someday, be a doctor—always hustling to some little job after school or on weekends. Make something of himself. But much too soon for those kind of thoughts. Just a girl. Just a boy.

In kitchen, grease stains on ceiling, on wall in back of stove.

8

Perpetual. Icons spattered by a subtle hand on the paper Gene had hung, kaleidoscoping to a thousand shapes as wide girl eyes concentrated on them, trying to fix something solid in her mind beyond the one unavoidable truth of her belly, to somehow return order to the baffling landscape of her life over which her mother's voice floated like an ominous fog.

—We can't tell him. After you're married and the baby comes will be time enough. By then, what's done is done. You'll be Clarence's wife, and your child will have a name. If your Daddy-Eugene gets mad, then I can talk with him, but now . . . it just frightens me to think what he might do. And what it would do to him. Lot of people started with a lot less. Just pray Honey, you're lucky he wants to marry you and you're both in love. What you were gonna do anyway, wasn't it. Everybody said so . . .

—Just a little harder, Baby, that's all. We got each other. I'll make good, for you, for our son. He's gonna be a son too, your looks and my smarts. Hey—what you frowning at . . . lips poked out a mile, you ain't pretty at all like that. Maybe he'll have to have my looks too. C'mon now Baby, ain't you gonna smile no more. Let me kiss those tears away. It's gonna be all right. We got each other Baby—it ain't like you to mope around. I like you smilin', laughin'. We're gonna go dancing soon, at the Roseland Ballroom, stay out all night. Old Daddy-Gene can't fuss now like he used to. We're almost married. Gonna be my girl now. Man, was he shocked. Bet your Mama had a hard time making him believe his little Martha had grown up enough to have a husband. But she sure has, she's gonna be my Baby always, aintcha' Hon. C'mon, dry those big, brown eyes. What are you lookin' so sad about.

At times in the small room Martha remembered as always being hers, just after undressing and feeling the cold slide of sheets over her bare skin, a feeling of finality enveloped her whole body, nothing so definite as a word or idea, but a wave of dizzying, impalpable images, succeeding each too quickly for any to be distinct, a terrifyingly real and unswerving motion that swept her far, far away until some part of her insubstantial as a ghost was removed, and from a distant wind-swept height it could look down pityingly at her body, which, frail and alone, she knew would never stir again.

Little red wagon you ain't got far to go. And there's fifteen cents at the other end. Fifteen pennies closer to them fine clothes and fine house and me and Martha the two biggest shots in town ridin' in our Lincoln.

—It won't hurt. You know I wouldn't do nothing to hurt you Baby. I know, I know your scared, but nobody's comin' in here, Uncle Carl's gone for the whole week, it's ours any time we want it till he gets back. Our first bed, Baby. C'mon, not so stiff, it ain't gonna hurt . . .

Mirror on high, old-fashioned bureau caught Clarence's head and shoulders for a moment. She looked away, fearing the weight that would soon press down on her stomach. Mirror, mirror on the wall—combing long, black hair, gazing at freckles she hated and two teeth too large Martha Beaver cried over when martyred she was in turn by the others, red-eyed as Mama brushed and oiled, telling how beautiful it was, silklike, falling over shoulders, but then braided so tight in strands to be grabbed and teased. How hard it was to be a little ugly girl. She wept inside and wanted DaddyGene to sing her to sleep softly . . . brush and hand so smooth, flashing white in mirror.

Somehow the hem of her skirt lay ruffled inches from her eyes. Funny, she had never noticed how untidy each stitch lay on underside of red-flowered material, how colorless cheap cotton dyed on one side seemed and laced edge of slip peeking over . . .

Teeth closed on rigid tongue, warm liquid spread in mouth, washing over gums, salty like gravy then unfelt as body split in two aching pieces. String hung light began to dance, her eyes fastened on it till they glazed over and began to sting not daring to look down over posy flung redness to where on all fours trembling he crawled into her bowels.

Rain, rain, go away, little Clarence wants to play. Scrawling moon faces on the steamed window, eyes that melted to tears and streamed down pane, face collapsing, spilling down in rivulets like wax man in a fire. Rain washing streets, sitting in quiet beads on fuzzy hair and oilskin coat as he stood framed in doorway. —You'll catch your death coming out in weather like this. Off shrugged he his coat and into warmth careful not to falter or shiver or seem to care about sodden levis pasted to his thighs or shirt damp on shoulders and chest, nor did Martha protest chill of quick coming together there in livingroom beside fireplace crackling, spitting like a hungry whip. Nobody was home.

Rain. Her whole body seemed drenched by a tepid, clinging rain. And it fell still, a puddle of moisture between their naked bodies. Oily, glistening on his chest as he moved away, caught in beads on his body hair, tiny globules like dew clumps she had seen early mornings in the grass. Urge to cover herself, to end her unexplicable first nakedness before a man, but powerful swell of tenderness made her leave sheets where they lay— half on, half off the bed, while with an ease she would have never dreamed possible, one leg was drawn slowly up, its toes caressing her calf and stopping midway on her thigh, fully conscious of Clarence's eyes watching the movement, and his bronze hand dropping slowly to retrace the path of her foot.

—I tell you I don't like it Freeda. Something wrong about this. All the sudden jumpin' up, thinkin' they's grown enough to marry. Martha ain't hardly stopped suckin' her thumb.

Secrets—a woman's secrets. Painful, kicking inside Freeda like all the grown and dead ones had. How much could she take, how much and how long could she hold them inside before they burst out wailing, demanding their due. Was it a sin . . . was she lying to Gene . . . did he know anyway . . .

11

would he forgive Martha . . . and even more, would he forgive her? She prayed the prayers of the damned, damned because her sin must continue, must go on at the very moment she kneels to ask forgiveness.

BLUE FOR A BOY, PINK FOR A GIRL, but I know, DaddyGene knows.

It shall be a boy, and his name shall be called Eugene.

Spring ended and was forgotten, but soon came again, again and again, repeating itself, forgetting in its own way, each time imperturbable, resigned as if nothing else, no other season happened.

From a height, from a blessed height another fell, wingless, full of grief, sorrowing even as he plunged down through the darkness.

Splat.

I'm goin' home to see my Baby, I'm goin' home, I'm goin' home.

You, goatman! Play for the children. Shyly from undergrowth hobbled the faun on wobbly hind legs. Cloven heels and tiny horns made him appear satanic, vaguely threatening, until his huge, empty eyes, limpid and bovine, turned to stare vacantly at the gruff voice, features slack in an idiot glance caught forever between something he cannot remember, and something he cannot forget.

Sweetly sounds pipe he lifts to lips. Faun plays . . . flute sad and fragile in brilliant afternoon air. At some point Centaur joined piping, his voice inseparable, one with mood, impelled upon spring day and minds that were listening. Sounds first, unintelligible murmurs, subdued, secretive like whispers, then kindling presence of the word, his voice lifted and pipe floating backward, receding to calm and stillness like an audible hush of all nature listening . . .

Whining did the faun complete, all had been said, played, night closed their eyes.

Fa la, fa la, faaa la la, la la, laa la.

Beat the drums softly, pipe the pipes slowly. Full of embalming fluid, waxen and gray, DaddyEugene in a flower draped box received his last and proper obsequies.

The next time I go in that place, they'll be carrying me.

Right you are, blasphemer, pagan, stay-at-home, Sunday-morning infidel.

Alas, we all knew him well. Family . . . community . . . church . . . Christian household . . . while not personally . . . everyone had a good word . . . saw fit in his own way . . .

High above the broken cobblestones of Casino Way, mounted on DaddyGene's shoulder his second grandson Edward swayed and sang with him.

Froggy went a courtin' and he did ride, uh huh, uh huh.

Going to hear the Sanctified, and watch Tiny dance.

We had to sneak, and sharing the secret for a day or a morning was half the fun. Like those wine bottles he hid I always knew where and Grandma Freed searched for, but I wouldn't tell and she knew I knew and told me how bad it was and how much it hurt DaddyGene and someday he might go away and it would be because of those straw-bottomed bottles tucked everywhere she couldn't find and perhaps cry till sometimes I trotted off and brought back one or two but felt sorry afterward and wanted to confess to him but instead only crawled on his knee to listen to him sing or snore till I too slept and forgot my guilt.

Nobody here don't care at all, drifting down Casino Way. Passing a peach tree whose plump fruit one day I would eat, every juicy one when big enough to climb the fence and with a stick chase away the nodding, red-eyed wolf dog.

Go tell it on the mountain, lifted down I was on wall opposite low brick building. *Tioga Street Sanctified in the Name of Jesus Christ Church* said glassed over scroll in homemade gold letters on black cardboard. Two large windows, that on

13

hot days had to be opened faced DaddyGene and me on our perch. Almost like being inside from where we sat, only pulpit invisible, words coming mysterious and faceless from a velvet-voiced throat beyond our view. Plain, yellow-gray plaster walls, cracked in places, decorated with posters, homilies, proverbs, maxims, bits of wisdom edited from every conceivable source. *Over the hill and everywhere.* Like mourners all were dressed in black, white shirts of men crackling in contrast beneath dark heads and necks, women's hair cropped and netted or veiled so each had a black, fat bag atop her head. All strangely lambent, benign, listening to the word and the melodious bursts of music punctuating prayers, scripture and notice reading. Passive nervousness. Crowd on the edge of something—orchestra tuning up, barrage starting, bull rumbling bewildered into a ring. Still point before the entertainment begins, before the blood and voice can participate.

Olay.

With a knock down, drag out, them dirty blues chord it began, quickly hand clapping and tambourines shrill jingle, jangle. Lord I've got good religion.

DaddyGene's big foot started tapping. From his inside pocket a flask was produced—guzzle, guzzle, click of metal on metal, spin and foot tapped faster. His jaws, large and square, moved fluidly in an exaggerated chewing motion. Wad of tobacco puffing out one cheek was reduced methodically, undisturbed by faster rhythm of foot and music. Two streams of thick oxblood spittle were expelled loudly onto cobblestones—splat.

—They's happy today, Eddie. Just started and listen to 'em wail. Love that stuff. These niggers fightin', cussin', and shootin' all week then comin' here like ain't nothing happened since the last time, all purty and clean, there's deacon Washington—Hey you black devil, hey you all you got the devil in there, he was drinkin' wine last night on the corner, yes he was—hey debil Washin'ton, sing your black butt off, go on knock yourself out, but don't put all yore pennies in the plate, we's got to get us some blood tomorrow—or tonight. Can't tell when you're going, and I ain't gettin' caught dry—splat.

—Work out sister Lucy, work out girl. She sure can sing can't she, boy. If I could just sit and listen to her everyday—splat—I'd stay in church. Get me a jug and lay back on a couple of them chairs and dig that fat sister chirp. Work out girl—splat. They's all gettin' heated up—watch 'em Eddie, they's gonna be dancing soon. Hey Tiny, hey you black elephant—splat—don't you feel the spirit yet?

Inside nothing but the shouting and chanting of the voice next to you could be heard. Let the King of Glory come in. And he did in top hat and tie, wearing striped pants and immaculate white, gold-buttoned spats on shining shoes. His teeth glinted brighter than diamond stickpin or rings big as quarters on his fingers, a slender, silver-tipped cane winked as it whirled enchanted in the air. Won't you come home Bill Bailey, won't you come home. Who is the King of Glory. Your host Baby, your toastmaster, and number one promoter of the biggest scene going. And they hallelujahed and wept and laughed with joy, shaking their heads—um um—eyes aglow like when Willie hits a grand slam or makes an impossible catch. Um—um. Let the King come in—tall and sparkling, heady and sweet—a brown eyed handsome man. Didn't it rain children, didn't it rain. And joy showered down, inundating the crude, crowded room and the bouncing hearts, and the tired, dark faces for a moment reflected the soul's smile.

Tiny started to sway. Barely perceptible at first, then his broad back rolled from side to side, first to the left then to the right, off time—a rhythm all his own—warming up—shaking his body's chains, palpitating inside each roll of fat, reviving the dead, hanging flesh so it quivered, so it jumped like so many nervous cats and in a moment on his feet, not lumbering as his tremendous bulk should move, but agile and smoothly coordinated like the lithe body of a shake dancer. Tiny up and feeling good. Arms out at either side, bent at elbows so fingers

15

pointed up trembling with joy, his head rolling from side to side, glazed eyes staring as if possessed by some miracle on the ceiling. He switched down the narrow aisle, wide buttocks wagging more supple than swivel hips of brown girls in tight dresses on the avenues. Twitching, shaking, light on his toes and balls of feet Tiny danced. In his world, in that moment he lived for, when the tremendous weight of his soft, spreading flesh would be cast off, and somewhere like a leaf or a gust of music he would be lifted by the wind, borne off lithesome on a cloud of grace.

Tiny's moment was DaddyGene's moment and in a subtle transformation became eternal in small boy wide eyed, excited beside him. One chubby hand slapped loud and gleeful on faded denim of old man's bibbed overalls, while the other seemed unable to rest in one place, rubbing his pug nose, finger deep in mouth, attempting to imitate loud pops of DaddyGene's fingers, sometimes just waving in the air.

The old man watched as sweat poured down Tiny's black cannonball head. Like a fat, heavy top spinning his motion slowed, gradually dying so the minute, barely touching point could no longer sustain the ponderous weight above it. Down crashing soon, its lightness and grace impossibilities that could never be repeated, that were only dreamed. Slower, slower, flush gone, sweat drying and cool on wrinkled, wet neck.

Old man intent, rubbing stubble of his still jaw. Regarding blood stained pavement between his knees. Tiny sprawled exhausted in a chair. Boy's hand stopped its rhythmic patting on his grandfather's knee. From nowhere an odd tickle made the old man cough, for an instant as if a shadow passed he felt a chill penetrate deeply to his bones though the sun never stopped. A low, concerted mumbling came from the small, crowded room, punctuated from the invisible corner with hollow throat deep exclamations. Wine that is my blood, stale loaf going bad of my flesh—will He answer to my name? Drew he the still glowing boy on his knee, studied smooth skin and undefined features for some trace, some hint . . . of what he wasn't quite sure, even why seemed not to matter, but the child, Little Eddie straining to understand what was being intoned on the other side of the wall, Little Eddie seemed to contain an answer. Not strong and loud like Little Gene or like himself, but something significant and unshakable that reminded the old man of a vast uneasiness, a youthful anxiety he believed he had forgotten. It never had been articulated, but he knew it was a question. A question he had to rise up tall to face, a question elusive and demanding that he felt would best be avoided. Nothing positive ever came of it, only a vague longing regret, and a threatening chiplike obstinacy that he never dared to disturb. Down his black beaver hat came, high crown covering Eddie's head, brim wider than round, soft shoulders it dropped to. Panic like a cat in a box, as small hands struggled to remove hat DaddyGene held lightly down. Blinking, flushed Eddie laughed, and his arms went around his grandfather's neck as hat came away, his tender skin excitedly aware of rough, abrasive feel of stubble chin. Hat in hands, sun glinted off DaddyEugene's bald pate, the waxen skin transparent, delicate in the golden glow. Huge hand circled boy sweeping him in one motion high back to shoulder perch. Down Casino Way lurching in late afternoon they went, a trail of rusty splotches behind them as a fresh wad was mangled violently in DaddyGene's jowls.

Splat.

To Freeda's reproaches and Martha's where have you been young man he down came and sadly watched giant suddenly tired disappear into livingroom followed by Freeda's slim, straight figure, His mother quickly took him upstairs for a nap chiding him gently for not telling her he was going off—even so, over her voice, and the stairs that squeaked, and through the door after it was shut, he heard angry voices from the livingroom.

Dearly beloved we have gathered here.

Splat—with a hollow rattle first earth bounced in tight balls on the wooden box.

He came that they might have life. Those three grown and two dead ones pushing up now other sprouts, big-headed brown boys.

Down the muddled tow path flanked by slow going bronze stream they ambled, neophytes unshorn of innocence boldly holding hands, flesh to flesh uncovered, tasted pure as sun on backs, grass damp squelching up between toes ticklish on undersides and backsides when they sat to picnic there beneath shade of spreading tree applehung and fragrant from early dying ones Psmanthe had kissed away they ate in silence as the earth turned languid as a lover in the morning.

—Time was when nothing, boy, nothing here but high weeds and wild grasses, hunted squirrels and whatever else moved right over there where you see them factories. Different then. Not so many niggers, not so many of anything 'cept what lived in them grasses and weeds.

—You be going to school soon. Listen to what they tells you Edward. But don't let 'em scare you, they scared me and all I done was learn to fight 'em and scare 'em back. If they tell you something you ain't sure about, just come right home and ask your DaddyGene.

A triptych of sorrow. Freeda flanked by Martha and her son-in-law, Clarence. In black a compact group, the two younger people obviously supporting pale, veiled woman who stared with precarious dignity outward, eyes fixed, reflecting gray of overcast sky dim like shadow of pride and fear so familiar when for years she had watched Gene go. So close the three yet each frozen in some vague distant posture as if the secret core of each being had moved out from the soul's recesses to circumscribe and isolate the figures, catching a pose, a gesture, an inevitable attitude or expression which made escape or penetration impossible, touching like stone figures twisted into some baroque fantasy, but distinct because the stone is unfeeling, cold, dead. Freeda felt herself sink into the soft earth, each shovel full of dirt landing heavily in the hole seemed to lower her deeper and deeper, sucked down into the vacuum of the earth's bowels. Little Martha skinny, trembling in an invisible wind, a sound of someone crying deep inside her floating up to her throat, pouring out as a sigh or sob each time she relaxed the pressure on her tightly drawn, bloodless lips.

Fall day, day falling to death rattle of dirt clods on wooden box, drum roll Clarence listened to oddly aware of black silk thrust through his arm, Freeda's weight rigid, stone cold like flesh not at all; black silk on a stone mannequin who when he moved would topple into the mud. House that Gene built small now, thought he, doubly awkward in the face of love and death. Returned he had to manless women, to their sorrow, to Daddy-Gene's wine-rotten death in the bathtub and his own slow dying in mirror eyes of woman he loved. To his sons already strangers, already were Eugene and Eddie straight limbed and silent.

For thine is the kingdom.

Words he could never say unless in a group—suddenly aware of Freeda's lips, white, flaking, even behind the veil obviously immobile. Dry eyed too, as if waiting, like swollen gray clouds overhead to pour down on the mound rising from the earth, wash it away levelling, secreting the grave, carrying gaudy flowers to oblivion.

If there be a season fit for planting, for the dead to be laid in rows, and faith to cover them over, and hope to wait for their return, if there be a season surely it is now. Now when rains threaten, earth is soft and the heart has sunk so low only a long winter's sleep will do.

Il pleut dans la ville.

Into rented black limousines they filed, doors slam shut—quickly windows are steamed and rain streaks the glass. Doggedly back and forth wipers sway, final, unswerving as pendulums. And on that great gettin' up morning there will be some who have never fallen asleep.

Back to the city, Allegheny County cemetery, green mound behind them.

Fa la la, fa la la, faa laa laa.

Goats nibbling at the blossoms—wilted, faded, brought by a bronze stream filling soft rutted earth. Bumblebees watch disdainful, no honey there they buzz, damn the scavenging goats, beards waterdipped and brown.

Fa la la, fa la, fa la.

Froggy went a courtin' and he did ride, uh huh, uh huh—

ONE

Of course it was raining. Eddie knew it would rain the day he left. He had a long walk down the hill. Gradually the slope levelled revealing more and more of the countryside to the slim figure in its tardigrade progress down from the gray walls. They were behind now. The gray walls, that gate always open and beckoning. Slowly on his shoulders it fell. Warm, silent rain, the rain some flower had been awaiting, the rain Eddie knew would come.

It was hard to believe he had passed through. Voluntary commitment, he was familiar with the concept, yes, it had appealed strongly to him, yes, it was probably the thing that had finally made up his mind. The gate is always open, and so it was, and so it was today as he walked through it across the gravel driveway and down the wet, green hill, rain on his shoulders. I am going home, again and again repeated somewhere inside his chest, from all of this I am going home.

The bus didn't come to the top of the hill. Grierson told him that just before Eddie left. Dr. Grierson, across the miles of mahogany in sacerdotal tones. —It won't be easy. We all know that. If anything has been gained here, it is simply part of yourself that for some reason or another you grew careless of and lost. We hoped at best to give you back to yourself. Grierson looked briefly over his shoulder through the huge, gray pane of glass, but when he spoke he knew all there was to know of the sky, —I'm sorry it's such a poor day. But then who are we to expect sunshine. For you, I'm afraid the clouds will hang heavy for quite a while. It won't be easy especially at first, we know that, don't we Eddie. We don't teach illusions here, do we; it will certainly be difficult at first, but then who are we . . . ending with a reminder that the bus stopped at the hill's foot.

The grass was wet and slippery, but resilient under his slow-going steps. He could see the sheltered stop deserted beneath him. Corrugated tin siding and overhang loud as in a few moments he stood under it. Grierson had said it wouldn't be a long wait; Eddie shivered and believed. Somehow that huge, gray pile brooding on the hill top seemed dependent on Grierson's simplest utterance. As if it too rested on implicit faith rather than concrete sunk into the earth. It *would* come soon winding up the road, its windshield wipers working inexorably. He must remember to go to the back when it came. Go to the back, slinking in as unobtrusively as possible. And if the bus became crowded he must not sit while a white man stood. Strange that after such an interlude, after being in limbo for over a year he would immediately recall the necessary facts. His whole effort would be to remain unrecognized, appear to belong, not to be a smart northern nigger. More than the hospital the thought of going South had frightened him. He had dreamt night after night of pursuit, torture, horrible death. Mutilated black bodies hanging from trees, smouldering on charred crucifixes, debowelled, blinded, chopped by axes. He had received whispered warnings from old people born in the South, read secondhand stories of horror retailed in Negro magazines. During his trip down he had spoken to no one, met no eyes until arriving at the small island of federal authority to which he had committed himself. In a rush it had all come back. How to be nothing. The months of self-intensity, of self-awareness faded with him as he shrunk inside the bus. If there was an eternity somewhere, even that would not be long enough to forget some things.

He rode alone in a corner listening to the rain. Gradually the bus filled, picking up knots of passengers as it lurched to a stop beside other tin shelters. Luckily it was a suburban express that skirted city traffic and congestion until it dipped off the expressway on a newly built extension directly to the rail and coach terminals. The bus had been too intimate for Eddie. Its steamed, rain streaked windows crowded in upon the occupants trapping the tentativeness and dissatisfaction each rider breathed into the stagnant air. The transparency of cheap plastic raincoats, hats pulled down, peaked rain hoods and scarves, collapsed, pointed umbrellas—all seemed to exclude Eddie, bareheaded, his suit damp and clinging to his shoulders. He knew the white woman in the blue plastic raincoat (probably something she could carry concealed in her purse) had stared over her thick, dark rimmed glasses. Beneath the blue hood her hair, gray-brown, was pressed to her skull and resembled a nest of snakes. A woman, unattractive, even repulsive behind thick round spectacles whose slightest whim, whose pleasure or displeasure was worth his life. He could hear the crackle of each movement she made. Irresistibly he felt glances steal from him, covert, destructive glances feeding on her ugliness. The heavy ankles, the shapeless bulge of thigh and hip under the translucent material. Her feet swelling red from the edges of clogs. How long had it been. A year at least, but certainly not brought to this, not brought as low as this. But thought too must die here. Plastic lisping, the crackling umbrellas lolling, shaking off bright beads of water from their loose fluttering ends were sharp beaked birds of prey responding to his thoughts echoing loud through the bus. If she would cry out, if she would point, he would be dragged out and murdered. Always that thought. That sleeping violence which he feared and courted in her female ugliness. A woman after a year. But even after that not her, not this one with her worm hair. I look because I do not love. Because I want her to know. I wouldn't have her even though she is a white woman. The first one. White Clara naked on his bed. He had been so confused, so tender, and afterwards the pasty, sour smell of her sex wouldn't leave his fingers. A dancer she was, strong limbed whom he had watched many times in the ballet school, sensing a dreadful heat and energy in her mysterious white flesh rippling beneath leotards. I love you I love you not, her cigarette breath and bad teeth, but she didn't care what you were, just men and women in the world, just men and women . . .

Alice, would she be waiting? Could she forgive?

Dear Alice:

I am going away. This is something I must do. I've tried to fight it by myself but now I know I can't. Maybe where I'm going they'll be able to help. I don't know what else to say. I just couldn't come to you the way I am, please try to understand. Why can't we touch without having it hurt? Your eyes Alice. I saw how far I'd fallen when you looked at me the last time. So much has happened to us. Please wait. Sometimes I believe this trip will make a difference. I'm afraid, but I think there is a chance. Do not forget. I love you.

Alice, the most beautiful dancer, would she forgive, would she remember . . . those distant things huddling naked in the frail warmth of his memory.

Another bus, another corner. A Greyhound scenic-cruiser, trembling, wheezing with life beneath him as its pigeon-necked driver gunned the engine. Eddie was early, and he sat alone suddenly chilled and tired. Already the morning had seemed years. If only sleep would come, he thought, if only I could draw it like a coat around my shoulders and close out the day. He huddled on the coarse grained seat, trying to adjust the headrest, twisting his body to take up the least space and still stretch out his long legs. The cheap suit now thoroughly soaked clung to his thighs, back and shoulders. If he moved the wet material away from his bare legs an icy draft curdled between the suit and his flesh. At least as the dampness chilled him, his body heat imperceptibly warmed it in return so he stopped avoiding his wet clothes and pulled them closer round him.

Mostly Negroes boarded the bus. Dusky farmers, big footed, big handed, foreigners emigrating to another country. Awkward

26

signs of what they expected and what they had left behind stamped them. The ill fitting, ill styled suits, florid bow ties and clodhoppers, the elegant fedora and coveralls beneath. Women in little girl dresses with slips hanging and too many colors. Hitching a ride on the freedom train. The strength and animal litheness of their bodies were revealed unexpectedly—a dark stare, a slim brown calf, hips and breasts thrusting against shapeless dime-store cottons, brutal hands. One day, in the city these things would be brought forth, what might have slept forever would be violently realized in the city's heat and passion. They took their places, shopping bags in hand, boxes, bundles, flour sacks, containers of every description piled overhead precariously in racks, flowing out, strapped and roped together in the aisles. Carting away all they owned to the promised land. A peculiar rootlessness visible in their eyes. Eddie knew what they would become. Could tell by the angle of a hat, or the color in a tie who would catch on and who wouldn't make it. Bright-eyes would be hooking on the avenue in less than a month. That big, black boy with the bandana around his throat would run numbers, beat somebody up then be found sliced or shot in an alley. An unsolved murder the police would never investigate. Eddie felt he had something to say, something they could understand. He wanted to roll up his wet sleeve, walk up and down the aisle like a preacher testifying. Somehow turn this load back, tell them the best they could expect and show the cost. But the Negroes sat sullen and suspicious, and Eddie shivered in his corner.

When she could walk, when both her sons were away at war, each morning Martha would go down to the gate and wait. She said she knew it would be morning when they returned, a bright, sunny morning, but she went down the bricked path every dawn rain or shine just in case. She would stand, still in her housecoat, either by itself or flapping below her man's old brown overcoat until the postman came. Not until she greeted him and took her letters when there were letters would she leave her post by the gate and return to the house. When she was sick for a week and confined to her bed, she wept even though her daughter Bette went and waited. One came back, Eddie, her youngest son; the postman in an envelope brought all that was left of Eugene, her firstborn.

She was different then. Even after the telegram from the war department she continued those morning vigils. Clarence couldn't stop her, and after her scenes, tears, and a cold, cold anger he feared in himself he stopped trying.

There had been three children who lived, but the man too loved most his eldest son. Eugene had been big like his father. He grew fast and rank, a strong hard-handed boy whose shoes had to be left outside at night. Huge, smelly things Martha would carry dangling like fish from their strings, holding her nose but laughing and loving the ritual when he would forget and she would point and shout, making jokes to the others while Eugene cringed and almost cried. It was just to be forgiven and for her to forgive. The tiffs they had. Him standing still, towering a foot over her head listening to her shrill angry voice and cowing from her threatened blows. But when she hit him, it really did hurt her more, his elephant hide and bones and buckles and she would cry.

—These shoes. From me, from my body came something that fits in these shoes. She loved the others, but it could never be the same. She had found and nourished different things in each, knew Edward or Bette could do things Eugene never could, but then how could she love everything about them, how could every moment, every action of theirs be an original and unrepeatable truth between mother and child. She was a child herself with him, and her man, still almost a boy when the first baby had come. She loved the child closely, intensely. It was something the father could only watch from a distance, sometimes jealously but usually simply in awe. Clarence would come and go, awkward in the face of their deepest magic; no matter how long he would stay away from home, he knew the child would remain an iron chain looped round them. Father and son grew up almost strangers, but loving and being loved by the same woman. After the war, Clarence stayed away and drank even more. Home at the end, his heart went bad and he died.

—Daddy, Daddy, Bette screamed at the dead man. Eddie was out, and her mother who moved very slowly then and always near sleep did not answer. Bette sobbed, deep, heaving sobs, suspending for a moment the hysterical screams she knew must come again as she moved across what seemed an endless space her fingers to stroke the dead man's brow. She shuddered at the touch, and screams burst from her gut shaking her body in wild convulsive heaves.

The two women couldn't lift Clarence. When Eddie came in they had only managed to straighten his body out and clean the floor around him. Eddie got a neighbor to help him place the corpse in the bedroom. After the funeral his mother stopped walking. She cursed her God and forsook him when she was delivered from her stroke.

All their relatives and friends brought food. Chicken, ham, cakes, pies, everything imaginable to fill the house. Then they came again to mourn and eat. During the viewing the house was filled with baking and cooking smells. From the kitchen rattling of pots, pans, and the eager, happy sounds of female activity drifted. Oh, we ate that week. We ate like kings. And all the niggers in the neighborhood greased with us. He was a fine man.

Eddie didn't look like his father; some older people said he looked just like his dead grandfather, but others said not at all. He was tall, but slim and fragile. He had his mother's high forehead with its taut, shiny skin showing his skull beneath and a palpitating vein that in anger thrust itself forward. Prematurely his light brown hair, wavy but thin, crept back from his forehead making its delicately molded surface dominate his face. Cheekbones high and prominent, brown eyes deeply sunken completed the impression of boniness; it was always an eggshell or skull people thought of. But when Brother Small saw him stepping off the bus, Brother thought of a scarecrow, or of a little boy in a borrowed suit. But it was Eddie all right, Eddie again after a year coming home.

—Eddie, Eddie Baby. Brother had his arms around the taller man before he could speak. When they stepped apart both were smiling almost to tears.

—Man, you been gone a long time. Eddie couldn't answer. He just looked at his friend letting his smile become something deeper. A vacant lot, brick throwing, chased down Dumferline Street, high on wine, high on pot, music, Mrs. Pollard's niece and back yard, chased down alleys.

—It's good to see you, Brother. Brother as always had his cap on. He wore his tan hustling jacket and pegged gabardine slacks flapped around his skinny legs. That was just how Eddie left him; it was as if he waited there all the time. But the wing tips were gone, walked out in a year's worth of sidewalk, replaced by a pair of canvas and gum casuals mostly rag.

—Times is been hard, Eddie. Like always. They were arm in arm now, and Eddie quickly looked up from the pavement. He met Brother's pale, red-rimmed albino eyes, disconcerted for a second, till the familiar warmth of the milky stare returned. His friend had probably been at the station all night.

Brother's jaw bulged with a wad of chocolate. He pushed a half-peeled Hershey bar towards his friend. As a bite melted to thick, sweet paste in his mouth, Eddie remembered how Brother used to eat chocolate all the time because he thought it would make him brown. But it only gave him pimples, big, ugly and white.

—You still eating that stuff? Brother grinned back remembering.

30

—Yeah man, can't you see, I'm gettin' a tan. He doffed his cap, presenting the bright dome of his cue ball head.

—Still going around blinding people you old skinhead. I used to think of that mirror of yours every morning when I shaved.

—Since when are you shaving every day? I knew you'd come back putting on airs. Least you got back outa there without no rope burns. They were quickly out of the terminal and moving towards the trolley stop.

—Shit, Brother, it's a holiday—the buses will be hours apart. Let's catch a cab home this once. I'm tired of buses anyway.

—Damn, you done come home with bread? If they pays you and feeds you down there, I might make that trip myself afterall.

—I got a couple dollars I saved, that's all, but it should get us home.

It was early morning and a cab was easy to hail. They moved steadily along Baxter Boulevard away from the center of town.

—Good thing we're going this way. Just look at the other lane. Bumper to bumper as far as I can see. Eddie didn't answer, and after a brief look, Brother understood. The wheels hummed monotonously, a kind of lulling silence that after a while wasn't heard. Eddie was worn out. Brother, after watching the stalled cavalcade of facelike chrome grills and head lamps, settled back content with his friend's quiet mood. They drove along a shelf cut into the hillside. Below them gradually terraced, clumps of houses, factories and warehouses tapered off and culminated in endless rows of smokestacks lining the river. A haze obscured everything but the broadest outlines. Above them, clearer it seemed, the chiselled stone and raw rock beyond cut off any view of the sky. They were an island whirring along an uncluttered gray channel, serene except for an occasional impatient bleat from the other side of the highway. Wearily the sun made an effort to poke through masses of stagnant gray clouds. Hanging over the river a brief patch of blue would glimmer then be swallowed up. Eddie was home and snoring; Brother slept beside him.

One more class. One more class, Thurley thought, and then perhaps a few welcome days of self and peace. Perhaps a chance to get to the book. This respite from class, the long awaited one when he would make the break, begin to write again. Still a boy, he thought, a dreamer still who chooses to believe. But afterall, those things long in coming often the best. The most complex mammals have the longest gestation periods, and what's more satisfying than the bowels erupting after a week's constipation. The door would open. Words hot, thick and pungent pour out so fast that his arm would grow weary transcribing before the flow from his brain diminished. A boy still. It is enough Sancho to believe, enough that I believe they are giants. And off to get bloody hell knocked out of me again. Thurley stood and went to the window. His office faced the new classroom building; he could see the two windows of lecture room 120. Soon the paths would begin to fill up. Students would file in disorderly spurts through the halls, in and out of the glass doors. Lecture room 120 will become alive. Thurley reflected on the collective mind he must meet, his own gross person and the tenuous threads of learning he must fashion into a screen between himself and the predatory audience. He comes that they may have light. All forty-five of them, forty-six including himself gathered like a pile of leaves into that room by forces too simple and too dizzying to conceive. Intention, motive, need, impulse—each day some odd assortment of causes conspired to throw them together. Or perhaps it was just the inscrutable, causeless principle behind all things that allowed so much disparity, so many cross-purposes, contradictions and antagonisms to settle regularly into intimate juxtaposition. Robert Thurley the preceptor, Thurley at whose feet this flock would gather. He turned his back to the still sparsely peopled walks, refusing any further mental comment to the invisible but powerful forces materializing outside his window.

The lawns seemed so placid, so cool at this afternoon hour. Often Thurley wanted to leave his brown, bookish cubicle and stretch out beneath a tree. Be a lolling undergraduate again, watch girls, read or write poetry, just sit quietly and exude his youth and beauty benignly as a light touching the passerby. But that was another day, another Thurley still firm fleshed and clean before alcohol had hollowed out his stomach. He took down the sleek black volume of French plays he was using for his course in tragedy. He would talk about Oedipus today, Oedipus from Sophocles to Cocteau. Swollen foot. Child abandoned in the forest—the good shepherds who raise him then lose him to the stars. Would they listen, would they understand? It's not something dead, not a fairy tale either, or a dirty joke to be snickered at. *Jocaste*—mother, wife, to the lost father, son, ghost. Ghost of the dead boy long abandoned. Do you see it all? The inimitable circularity, the gruesome beauty *Oedipe* cannot bear to look on. The scream, the scissors a jagged cross in his hands. But even so, we endure, we go on though we lean on the thin arm of our shame made manifest, though we are led by the irretrievable fruit of our sin.

A thousand sailors. The love call of their brutal laughter, the caress of their angry blows. And yet I would go each night, humbly to seek peace, to unhungry the animal that must feed on love. No substitute I've found. Oyster shells, sawdust on the floors. Will they understand?

With unseeing eyes Thurley regarded his watch. It was necessary to repeat this purely instinctual motion to really check the time. He did have a minute, enough time to extricate his concealed half-bottle of Southern Comfort from the bottom drawer and longingly wet his lips. A gulp, then the fiery thread thrilling into his maw. Sometimes it could be so good. It could make the difference between cowering in this cramped space and striking out boldly to meet the denizens of 120. Thurley raised the ungraceful bottle again. He knew, his blood knew it would not be easy today. Many of his students would have left early for the holiday and those who remained would be either helplessly restless or overtly pugnacious. And Thurley would meet them at feeding time. Sometimes the impending struggle made him cold, unfeeling, but often heavy, uncontrollable moisture would slick him beneath his clothes. Even after so many years, he was like a baby, wet like a baby when he met them.

How far was it across the quad? How many steps to the other side, to 120 and the forty-five? Addice, Anderson, Bennett, Bond, Bowie, Boyd, Carr . . . The girls near the front, their dresses unnecessarily high, knees shapely, the calf muscle bulging pleasantly where it crosses and spreads against the thigh. Watson, West, Westbrook, Williams, Windsor. How shall he presume? The first step out of the chair close to impossible. Thurley tilted the bottle again. From the golden-brown triangle it formed in one corner the liquid lapped to meet his tongue. It lay hotly in the space between his lips and teeth, burning as he slowly drew it in swills across his gums and down into his throat. It could be so good. Clearing the space, leveling the phantoms that had gathered outside his window. It would be difficult today, but the show must go on. It was simply a question of the stronger will. His or the forty-five. What he loved most he must protect even to the cost of his own blood. If he gave up, if he submitted to the intimidating, hulking indifference, it would respond like a dog when it knows someone fears it. The coward would rise, curl back its lips and attack.

In a hazy moment he was perched cockily on the corner of a desk. Since the desk sat on a raised platform he could peer owlishly down at the forty-five over the steel rims of his glasses. But the chill was becoming overbearing. In spite of the whiskey, in spite of his resolve he felt the ice, the thickly packed layer after layer that he must walk upon to reach them. He had blithely begun; without trepidation or fear he launched into the glacial atmosphere. Yet even the way they responded to the roll call was cold. The tone of each voice belligerent, almost an afterthought rather than a reply to Thurley's voice tolling names. *April 20*. Many gaps, many little x's in the close columned book. Each absence one x, a tiny scarlet letter Thurley duly had recorded. But for him, for the teacher something etched much deeper. They don't care, don't give a damn about what I'm saying. It's a requirement, an obstacle to be gotten over with least bother. So they come and demonstrate their disdain. They wait for me to play the fool, to live up to the stories that circulate about me. A clown, a showman, who, if they're patient, they may see pull some colossal blunder, involve himself in one of his periodic scandals which they can say they saw enacted live onstage. Thurley teetered, dangerously close to falling from the edge of the desk. He experienced the profound vertigo of absolute solitude in a crowd. The eyes of his students were glazed over, and they saw nothing. Their lips were sealed, they spoke nothing. Their ears were clamped shut, and they heard nothing. Thurley veered away from his carefully planned lesson. Like so many beautiful white birds settled on a lake it had been till a sudden noise shocked them into abrupt confused flight. He saw white forms soar, float up and scatter—gone. No one had read. No one had the slightest interest in what he so desperately wanted to convey. The absurdity of it all, him intoning from his rock to the deaf multitude. His life depended on what he said, on how he defended his cause, but the jury was composed of wood. Mocking images of life diabolically set out to confront him. In their unpreparedness, the class formed a solid block against him. If someone had read, had understood, they would be too aware of the battle lines that had been drawn to cross them. It was their will against the professor. They would combine and by their very weight nullify his accusing effort. The forty-five would smother his just one little candle to plunge 120 into comfortable darkness.

But still Thurley had to speak. Calmly and with the fatal

poise of resignation he was ready to begin his final speech. Of course in its futility and detachment, its introspection and blindness, it had to be a soliloquy. He slid from the desk, nearly losing his balance and evoking a snicker, to stand before them. Without realizing the ridiculousness of the motion he hiked his trousers over the protruding slope of his belly. For him, this slight adjustment and the quick combing motion of his fingers through his sparse hair served to restore whatever dignity had been lost in his awkward dismounting of the perch. A cigarette was the final prop. In a moment one hung suavely, pasted to his lower lip as he fished through his pockets for a light. Those closest to Thurley sensing his helplessness had already begun to smile, and a low murmuring from the classroom's rear was becoming audible. To Thurley it was the sound of ice cracking. It was his unsteady footing giving way to plunge him into the numbing depths. It was the earth moving as gigantic glaciers collided. His hands hung at his sides, and the limp cigarette dropped from his mouth as he spoke again. This time it was word unfettered, the pure, intense content of a moan articulated. Thurley's mind began to cry. It wept for things only the mind that has suffered can penetrate and know. Dry-eyed he tried to hold them in their chairs, tried to make them see what he saw, comprehend the gray annihilating cloud that was settling upon them. He was as usual eloquent in his grief and perfectly incomprehensible to the students. At last he settled for laughter, for their jeers and grins at him and his throes of ineffectuality. He released them and his hold on the truth by transforming their uneasiness and his fretful being into the hollow composure of laughter. He was the prancing butt, he was the grimacing clown they could crucify. In a flash it was over; they growled and bounded after him, their teeth sinking into his rubber flesh, their claws tearing away his limbs that stretched and popped like bubble gum. They destroyed him and in the passing of their wake 120 was quiet.

Thurley thought of the sea. Of a beautiful young sailor

who had robbed and beaten him. It was a beatitude. A scene for Raphael to paint in his reds and blues.

Thurley replaced the forgotten book of plays in his briefcase. Before his eyes swam *Jocaste*'s preternatural scarf. Outside the walks had filled. Thurley found another cigarette and finally discovered his matches on the desk behind him. It took several tries to light it, but when the smoke finally curled through his nostrils and carried its mist into his lungs Thurley sighed a heavy sigh of relief. As his gaze lowered from the ceiling he caught the image of a figure half hiding in the doorway. Before he realized what the impression meant and could turn again to find who had been watching him from the doorway, the sound of running footsteps resounded in the marble hallway shattering the stillness. He could only tell that it was a girl in cleated loafers, and from the soft sound distinguishable before the shoes' staccato echoes, she had been crying.

It was a beautiful piece of jewelry. Green stones set in quincunx on a plain gold frame.

—It was my mother's, he said. It was my mother's, Thurley said to the boy sitting on the edge of the bed.

—She gave it to me many years ago and I want you to have it now. How she would have died again to see the bony, black creature reach out its hand closing its long fingers to make the pin disappear. Like catching an insect they clamped so quickly.

In a moment the boy was gone, clutching his treasure, afraid almost to look at it, to open his hand until it could be dropped in some glass jar to behold. Through the dark streets he ran, his prize hot in his hand. The stars were eyes, but tonight they were laughing.

I really loved the little nigger thought Thurley sitting later alone in his study. It was the den of an epicure, heavy with the possession of things. A Munch, mostly skull, hung over the artificial fireplace, blackened bronze statuettes of classical horses and gods crowded the room, jade figurines, Buddhas with empty laps for receiving incense, a marble topped table, a rococo inlaid and gilded writing desk over which hung El Greco's *Cardinal Guevara,* all contributed to an impression of repleteness but at the same time were isolated in their hard individuality. He smoked, satisfied with the silk against his skin, with fragrant wreaths floating above and around him. Night seemed always full of forget, full of promise, after a satisfying physical interlude, that life would continue to be played out in half-light, in pleasant bodily fatigue to which sleep would bring completion.

From a corner an oboe related a lugubrious theme. Thurley knew the oboe was the sound of death.

We had eaten together. Huge chunks of tenderest steak. The little black boy all eyes and silent but for his chops working furiously. As if it would disappear before he had finished. Music then too, but lighter, violins and candles subliminal, but certainly what he would remember later when hot meat taste had gone. Somehow everything.had led into those moments, as everything floundered ungainly into these. My guest: a gamin, urchin, pickaninny, street boy to partake of the fatted beast.

On North Street I found him. Dirty of course, skin of cocoa, sheep hair curling into a thousand dusty beads. Ask of him a question. Traveller in another country you see. I would like a pack of cigarettes. Shy of course. Timorous, ready to run or kick, to cry out if approached too quickly, if affronted or embarrassed by the sudden intrusion of huge mass of my white flesh speaking. He answered from behind a bush, one foot and hand still in the undergrowth anchoring his slowly emerging voice. A dog slinked by. The boy's brown eyes followed pit-pat of the mongrel's feet on the pavement as it skirted them tail between legs. I am not afraid now tone, slight smirk as if to say, my world, he pointed mumbling –Right around that corner mistah.

–I'm looking for a cab, and I'd hate to miss one by moving off the main street, son, if you could please run and get cigarettes for me you can keep the change, producing a half dollar.

The brown hand hesitated then was thrust abruptly forward, unfolding like a dirty flower. Suffer the children to come unto me. Away quickly walking, then trotting towards the corner all long legs and stick arms dangling he diminished trailing one clenched fist.

The oboe receded. Two voices in duet taking up the theme, antagonistically opposed in counterpoint, miles distant, irreconcilable. Male, female.

Thurley unseated himself, trailing scarlet folds of dressing gown through the dining room, then entered his small kitchen the red silk billowing around him as he knelt to remove a pat of butter from the floor. Things were still piled on the sink. Pots, pans, the Dresden china with its thin blue bands, silverware caked with remnants. A plastic tray bent by firm pressure from both his hands expelled with the sound of chicken bones cracking triangular pellets into an ice bucket. He only half-filled the airtight receptacle knowing this would suffice for his final gin and tonics of an evening.

In religion an aesthetic Catholic, in politics a passive Communist, in sex a resigned anarchist. He filled his tall glass. His check was late, spent anyway, but late. There was some satisfaction in possession if only for a moment, in dispensation if only a token, salutary displacement where he pleased. Butcher, Baker, Candlestick Maker and Hermann.

—Ya, sure docktor herr professor Thurley. Ya, ya you buy here things, Hermann has much to choose from you buy all here professor docktor sir, pay later, anytime. You would honor me herr docktor. And he did have it all. Gray grainy bottles of bitter lemon, pâté, smoked salmon, crab meat, lobster and shrimp canned of course but everything from Scandinavia, Germany, France, Russian caviar, Polish vodka and of the Herr Docktor's patronage an irreducible debt.

Traffic swooshed by infrequently on North Street. He stood on the pavement dressed in a wilted lightweight suit, stylishly olive hued doing its best to disguise the weary obesity his body moved irresistibly towards. The pants had slipped below his paunch. If one comes I will hail it and wait till he returns. Somehow I'll get him in it too.

After the meal the boy had been sleepy. His big eyes drooped and the weight of the strang⁻ white man's house tired his meagre shoulders. —Mistah Bob, I wanna go now. Thank you very much for the food, but I think I better go now. The room full of objects cowed him. Made him start as gazing from thing to thing each one momentarily seemed to measure him in return. The buddha with the empty belly, the skull death-colored staring from the wall. At times they spoke aloud, but at others moved out of his range of hearing and vision to continue their malevolent life free of him and the man reclining on the couch. When they spoke it was distinctly, but in a language incomprehensible and of things he wished cloaked in silence.

Thurley too heard voices: Crime in the streets: City shocked by vice exposé. Well known university professor arrested soliciting male partners for unnatural acts. Amid furor President Goodfellow announced immediate dismissal of offender promising at the same time masculinity oaths would be administered to all faculty members, women included. The professor was charged today in morals court on sixty-nine counts. The star witness, a vice squad agent who disguised as a twelve year old Negro boy permitted himself to be molested. Pictures on pages five, ten, twelve, thirteen, seventeen, twenty.

I loved the little nigger, Thurley thought drinking alone. If love comes into this cluttered world, it is in the quiet space between orgasm and not orgasm.

The thick blue book was opened. It was a diary, album, commonplace, letter, scrap, miscellany optimistically inscribed on its opening leaf *These fragments I have shored.* Thurley wrote: April 21, Easter Eve: Consummation—the momentary reconciliation of black and white in the heat of coition. I have paid for it with her jewel of great price.

The remark completed a page. He pondered its contents,

dwelling a moment on the last entry, then turned the leaf with his right index finger. The new blankness was oppressive. Two wide, long sheets of heavy paper blandly white. A mirror, a dark, white mirror, refusing his image. Hopelessly confused but somehow ineluctably true the metaphors danced and persisted. Dark-white, transparency-opacity, returning-refusing his image. The strands of experience, the rainy days and nights, mistakes that would go to fill up the pages. Thurley saw as far ahead as he could see. Forever—he would get up at eight, go to his brown office and catch up on the previous day's correspondence, carefully filing away any new mail till the next day. He would teach from ten until eleven, then again two to three. Between he would lunch with Noonan, at Dante's more than likely where they could have draught Michelob. He would leave his office at five going directly to Hermann's to shop, always hurriedly, probably taking a cab if one could be found because Hermann closed promptly at five-thirty. He would be home and in a chair with a drink by six, reading, writing or just drinking except every other Wednesday when he lectured at the art school, or the approximately once a month invitation to dinner by one of three friends who since unknown to each other never alternated their invitations very satisfactorily. Three times in one week, or else not one for months. This schedule varied by an odd faculty meeting, rare sorties to Midwestern conferences, a movie, a play or concert was Thurley's life. When he projected it in his imagination almost every distinction dropped away from the events. It was undeniably true—only the most elemental events of this routine called up any response. He recalled as vivid and substantial only weariness as his body came to consciousness in the mornings, the anxious, ridiculous dash to Hermann's late each afternoon, and finally fear as he dropped into bed at night that the booze would wear off before morning, that he would start up wide awake before dawn in a pool of wet, rumpled bedclothes.

Professor of Comparative Literature. B.A. Harvard. Ph.D.

Sorbonne, Oxford. Somewhere certificates pasted in full-of-truth blue book. At points we diverge, essential points in fact. Always a clean white page to begin on. *Où sont les neiges*. The boy had been strangely unreluctant. Although detached, even cold in a numb, childish fashion, the boy had willingly submitted. First his shoes, then his socks and trousers pulled off by the Doctor's trembling white hands, his priest hands moving of themselves, mechanical but infused with timeless primordial mystery that guided his fingers with a logic more powerful and comprehending than his own being. The flesh presented to his lips, staleness of his own groin floating up to meet him as he knelt. Breath of a dying wino. With this kiss I thee wed, the lean black bridegroom puff of veiled white beside him arm curled into his as they stood rigid with grotesque, confectionery smiles atop the pyramid of cake. Stale cake toppling then as knife keenly enters collapsing with a wheeze the creamy icing. He gave of himself in grudged, thin spasms. The hierophant rose on stiff knees.

The eyes still said I want to go home. That though you have done with me, and I am glad you have finished, I have never begun. The boy stood, his ashy legs quivering, dropping his eyes to stare at the glistening stem of his sex. It too pouted, tipped by an opaque bauble like a runny nose. He bent and gathered his clothes, too grimly absorbed to notice his host as he left. Too quick the host thought, too quick and now the irreparable silence. A swift shadow of fear across the boy's face directed Thurley to his middle, and his white hands buttoned clumsily the fly that still gaped. He tried to smile as he completed this act cursing inwardly the little Italian tailor who had repaired the trousers that hot summer in Naples. He hated his own coarseness, his lapses into natural ease that always produced loathing rather than sympathetic recognition, revealing the brute instead of soiled angel he wished to appear. He had shocked the boy. Ironically the enormity of everything else had simply disarmed him, made him passive. But the sound of the toilet flushing, Thurley's forgetfulness, haste and fumbling with the row of buttons revived a familiar, sordid world of old men, alleys and forbidden deeds. In spite of music, chocolate and the conciliatory, maternal concern of Thurley's voice for another hour the boy remained rigid inside his shell. The last desperate act had won at most his hand to grab the jewel before he tore off into the night.

Thurley knew Eddie Lawson was coming home. It had been a long time, so long that he feared their reunion and had resolved to avoid him. But as the day came closer, he could not conceal from himself the necessity of another meeting. The first and only time he had seen Eddie had been in another city, the seashore. He couldn't remember the name of the bar where it had begun or the exact date of their brief encounter, but some low, sweet jazz, something by Miles Davis, perhaps it was *Green Dolphin Street,* blended with the bar's smoke and darkness and gave to the night's events an identity that would always live inside him.

—You see being a white man you just wouldn't dig. The Negro had leaned close to the white face of his interlocutor. He had swept his sunglasses with a limp, magnificent flourish of his wrist from his sweating face. The Negro was green in the barlight, his thick lips pouted purple. —I don't mean no harm but it's as simple as that, baby. His voice was artistically modulated, from throaty tones to the high almost female whines of emphasis.

Two more drinks were set down. Thurley's white hand dipped then bloomed fluttering green. There was nothing more to say. Afterall the Negro knew, he just couldn't dig.

It had all passed now. That wet dishrag slap of sensation across his face as Thurley had entered the bar less than an hour before. Arctic Avenue, just a few blocks off the boardwalk, from the ocean that he somehow felt he could still hear. It stank, the onion, piss, stale beer stink of every dive in every city three thousand years of civilization had produced. It stank and was full of racket—jukebox music, glass thumping and clinking, chairs dragged, feet stomping, the cacophony of human voices. A din striking him as solidly as the fetid musk of body heat when he entered the door.

It was strange how the darkness made no difference. Thurley still felt hot and exposed as a boiling lobster here in spite of the bar's obscurity. The barfly who had quickly approached him to bum a drink had made his entrance easier than he expected, but their roles had already begun to change. Always like that. The giver always unable to stop giving so that the very act of giving becomes a dependence. Why always like that? Why not smooth and pure? One drink accepted, consumed, fini. Back to your corners. But never like that, even this loudmouthed scavenger deep inside him already and him powerless because he gave first. The Negro's breath again. His mouth yawning for ages before the first word. Purple gums dangling below his upper lip. The horse teeth.

—But we's all bruvers anyway, ain't we? I mean to say under this, he pinched the green flesh of the back of his hand. —All the same is what I mean. He gulped the Guckenheimer's, sputtering as he coughed, wiping his chin with a huge yellow handkerchief produced from nowhere, I ain't nobody's fool you know.

Thurley smiled and turned away. He caught the bartender's eye and in a voice he felt condemning him as he spoke asked for the washroom. It had a sign, but the little electric *M* had burnt out. The door whined on its taut spring then slammed behind him with a furious swoosh. He read the inscriptions. Always tell most about a place by coming here. Not simply how clean, but what kind of people frequent. Here only the crudest sorts. The sensual purity of African art. Phone numbers, names, numerous highly stylized representations of the phallus, something that was either a mouth, cunt or arsehole. He shook himself carefully before re-entering the arena.

It was obvious they all knew. He was surprised one of the more desperate hadn't followed him in. After all why else would a white man be here. He remembered his shame at his body on the beach. He was sensible enough to keep it covered, but the others, the flabby, red-fleshed, shameless others baring their dying bodies. Like sores or wounds out there in the sand. Wrinkled, blue-veined. They made him think of birds, not soaring, graceful kinds, but wobbly, fat bodied anachronisms with atrophied wings dropping feathers as they waddled, smelling of death. Some went by in chairs pushed by straw-hatted Negroes. Some of the chairs were motorized and nothing seemed more majestic to Thurley than a straw-bonneted black boy atop one of these pleasure barges guiding it along the boardwalk. Herr professor was here because he wanted a ride, and so what if they knew it.

The bar had grown more crowded. The Negro had moved off, too drunk even to capitalize on his luck, but others had come. Thurley resumed what he thought was his place by the appearance of a half consumed whiskey sweating on the counter.

—Hey man, you got the wrong drink, that's my friend's drink. Thurley turned towards the sound of the voice. He saw a face, ghostly lurid even in the half-light. The face was shaded by a cap tightly pulled down beneath which two eyes fixed him in a milky stare. He realized it must be a white face, whiter even than his, but distorted into crude Negroid features.

—Excuse me, I left one, and I thought this was it.

—Well it ain't. It's Eddie's. The face abruptly turned away relieving Thurley of the task of finding pupils in the glazed, opaque eyes. He inched away from the mistaken glass ordering another drink.

—No offense, man. The voice had moved from its stool and was now close over his shoulder. You know how it is though, everybody out here trying to get something. Just didn't want no mistake. Thurley listened without looking up, nodding slightly when the voice nudged him. Finally he knew he must speak, that he must say something or the eyes would cut into his back.

—I understand . . . it's nothing. Forget it, won't you have a drink? The eyes made no response, nor the voice, yet Thurley felt clearly and distinctly the man's reply. He felt it in the pit of his stomach.

The hand reached out, long fingers of the same unreal glowing flesh wrapped round the glass, thirstily Thurley thought, as if they drank before the whiskey reached his mouth. The man smacked his lips loudly and grinned. —Thanks Boss, you're all right.

They were side by side now. The albino stranger talking rapidly, passionately in a dated bebop idiom. Not only this language, but his worn hipster clothes showed him to be vintage. Thurley noticed all these things, his shabbiness, his lisp, but most of all the pure ugliness of the man's face gutted by pimples and scars like craters in the garish light. His disgust was aroused by this ugliness, by asthmatic sniffing and wheezing between sentences as the albino labored to say something before the catarrh up from his lungs thickened in his throat forcing him to spit down between his legs. The fitful sing-song voice, the human weakness and need that forced the man to serve up his unpalatable being to other men frightened and excited Thurley as the dish was pushed towards him.

—It ain't nice out here is it, man. It's even hard to breathe. I mean look, every cat in here has got his bag. A bag, that's what life is, a bag. Born in one, carried out in one. Spend the rest of the time gettin' tied up in others. Everything's a bag. Take my friend Eddie for instance. Eddie's a smart cat, but he got so many bags he don't know where to begin. I try to tell 'em, there's only one thing for it. But he just keeps fighting off one so he can get in another. All these cats in here. Ain't one of 'em that ain't in a bind. They's all in that big black bag, and that's enough to kill 'em. You know what I mean?

Thurley nodded, watching as the white aproned bartender mixed a drink. Thick arms, shadows accenting the twisting cordlike veins, violently shook the tin container and clear plastic

46

measuring flask shoved into its neck. Arms like carved black logs trembled with force, rattling the ice and liquid to a storm that foamed out thick and softly crimson from the strainer into long stemmed cocktail glasses. The albino was motionless, his little eyes now opaque, now squinting red and piglike as they caught the light. He seemed to be searching for his reflection in the dim mirror behind the bar. Something shadowy and elusive there behind the glittering bottles, metal and crystal fixtures that would relieve him if only momentarily from the sure image of his ugliness. When the albino spoke again, Thurley felt it was to this ghost, and because of that Thurley listened more closely.

—You know Boss, sometimes I'm scared for Eddie. There's only one thing for it, but he keeps fightin'. A man can't be but so strong. His tones were low, pathetic, he seemed to realize Eddie was the only way of telling his own story. He reached out and took the abandoned drink. His eyes met Thurley over the rim of the glass, smiling a chilly devil smile of recognition.

—I don't know where Eddie is. I guess he ain't comin' back. Why don't we go have some more somewhere else. The blatant, assured tone was of command. He had swallowed his own ugliness and Thurley could not refuse. It would all be simple now, he was obviously a weekend tramp in the weekend city with no place and no one to go to. There would be the night and morning would follow, then the albino would go shake the sun off his shoulders and disappear into another dark cave, sick to death of his ugliness till another like Thurley would come and receive it. They walked out together, touring from bar to bar till staggering and leaning on each other they wound their way out of the Negro district towards Thurley's hotel arm in arm.

—Brother, Brother. Thurley alarmed at the sudden intrusion stopped on the dark threshold of the *Empire Arms*. The albino straightened himself, pulling from him, sidling away from the vestibule door. All Thurley could think of was please no trouble as he extended his arms to steady the listing figure of the drunken albino. Groping in the immense distance between them he suddenly realized his own state.

—Please no trouble. A man had emerged from the shadows. Please no trouble. The man ignored Thurley, moving straight towards the albino who collapsed in his arms.

—Brother, are you O.K., man? He was so intent on holding up his friend that he didn't notice the white man disappear behind the vestibule's outer door. Thurley watched through frosted glass as the two figures stumbled gutterwards, the albino doubled over, dragging his feet, and the slim stranger hunched in the effort of supporting him. He could only see blurs of movement, something that seemed one body violently attempting to sunder itself. From the dark huddled mass a pendent bulk lurched three times, long, hard spasms then slowly was lifted upright. In slow motion one shape sagged slowly to the concrete, lolling dizzily in a slumped sitting position supported under the armpits by the other figure. Slow, methodical movements, exaggerated and prolonged like some surreal ballet. Thurley felt the rising and falling of his own chest, the damp glass pressed against his forehead. Something squirmed warningly in his gut. Both men seemed now to be sitting quiet and serene on the curb. Nothing to fear. No trouble. Suddenly the pane of glass separating them was cold and officious. With a feeling of shame and embarrassment Thurley flung open the door and stepped into the cool night.

—Is he all right? The stranger glanced up, but didn't reply. Thurley knew there was nothing to say, but the knowledge only made him more anxious to speak.

—I didn't know he was sick. One minute fine, walking with me, then he heard you calling, and when he turned around, it was all I could do to keep him from pitching down the steps.

—Just leave us alone, will you please, mister?

—Aw Eddie, he's all right. He's my man. Bobbie baby is swinging. Brother's speech was cut by a series of rapid hiccups.

The sharp, explosive sounds wouldn't stop, and he gasped for breath while Eddie beat on his back with the flat of his hand. Finally after one long spasmodic heave, he was quiet; his chin dropped to his chest and his arms dangled loosely between his splayed legs. Running down his pasty face were tears of exertion.

—Brother's not going anywhere tonight mister so you might as well shove off. He paused, glaring a threat, —Does he owe you anything?

—No, no, nothing. I'm just concerned that's all. He seemed a nice fellow. The two men measured each other in the streetlamp's half-light. Thurley felt cornered, caught. As if some raw, blazing light had come on exposing him. But he could see no more of his antagonist than the vague slim form he had discerned through the glass.

They are tableaued in the arc of a streetlamp. Hotel façade in background. Thurley takes one step then halts peering down at the albino slouched in the gutter. Drunken singing floats out of the night. Thurley kneels and retrieves Brother's cap from the sidewalk where it lies half-in, half-out of the streetlamp's yellow arc. The stranger accepts it, giving the soft felt quick swipes with his hand, then turning it, pats and shapes the material, his fingers extended into the crown. He covers Brother's naked pate and rises fully conscious for the first time of the white man who sways and totters above him.

THURLEY: Are you sure he'll be all right?

EDDIE: As O.K. as he'll ever be.

THURLEY: May I do something to help? (Silence as Eddie looks deliberately from the gutter to the white man and back again.)

EDDIE: You don't get it, do you mister? You just don't get it at all. What a fool you look like standing there asking if you can help. You've already helped him enough. Now get outta here before a cop comes along and we get arrested for bothering you.

THURLEY: You don't understand.

EDDIE: You're right about that. I sure don't. That's why I'm here with my half dead friend in a gutter, cause I don't understand. Why you won't leave us alone. That's what I can't understand. He can't go any lower, there's nothing left to do to his soul so why won't you just let 'em die, let 'em at least take his body to the grave without the prints of your lily-white hands all over it. Go away.

THURLEY: (Moving back, shaking his head.) Please, listen to me. That's not the way it is. I haven't come to prey on him. I want nothing from him it would hurt him to give.

EDDIE: It wouldn't hurt him to give anything. He'd give it all for another drink or a smoke or whatever you had to offer him. That's why he's dying, why he's . . .

THURLEY: No, no, that's not true. We wound up together because I'm like him.

EDDIE: Because you're hungry and the price of nigger meat is cheap.

THURLEY: Watch him, he's trying to stand up. (Both grab at the rising albino, steadying him.)

BROTHER: Hey Eddie, stuff and booze don't mix or I ain't as nasty as I used to be. (He hiccups once.)

EDDIE: Shut up man, shut up and stand up straight. We have company. Get your hands off him white man.

BROTHER: That's Bobbie-baby. Bobbie's just giving his man a hand. He's my ace.

THURLEY: How do you feel?

BROTHER: I ain't bad, but it's kinda hard to catch a breath and my heart's going like a bat outa hell.

EDDIE: Get your hands off him! (Eddie jerks Brother away from Thurley, shoving the white man's hand from Brother's chest. His own arm recoils.) Filth, white filth.

50

BROTHER: Eddie, Eddie, what's wrong with you man? He's only trying to help.

EDDIE: He's helped enough.

BROTHER: C'mon man, come out your bag. I tell you this is my friend. (He leans, or rather totters towards Thurley. His arm goes around his shoulders. Eddie steps back, glaring at them both, a single vein palpitating wildly in his forehead.) —C'mon Eddie. (Brother circles his free arm towards Eddie in an expansive gesture of reconciliation.) —Brothers under the skin man. Bobbie's all right. (A policeman appears from the darkness. Tall, thick bodied in blue.)

POLICEMAN: What's going on here? These fellows giving you any trouble. (The men separate, Brother drawing towards Eddie.)

THURLEY: No officer, everything's fine.

POLICEMAN: Well, let's get it off the street. These niggers know where they should be after dark. There's room enough in that nigger heaven down there. I suggest you go indoors, sir. They're not to be trusted, one minute grinning at you, the next putting a knife in your back and their paws in your pockets. I know 'em like a book. You fellows shove off. (He disappears out of the arc.)

EDDIE: Your friend has nice friends doesn't he, Brother?

THURLEY: He spoke for himself.

EDDIE: I didn't hear you contradicting anything he said. Let's get out of here Bruv, before he comes back. He won't be so nice if he finds us still here bothering this gentleman. (He spits.) God, sometimes I wish for that knife, and a row of fat white backs.

BROTHER: You're in that crazy bag man. He don't mean it Bobbie, he don't mean it at all.

EDDIE: If you believe me, mister, if you believe that I hate you to the bottom of my soul, you'll be as close to the truth as you'll ever be. (Thurley stands motionless in the light's glare. He only blinks watching as words are flung like stones at him. A whistle blows. Eddie grabs his friend by the elbow, they move off quickly, slouching towards the shadows. A cat meows, there is a clatter of garbage can lid falling. Whistle again. They are almost running. Brother looks back once, halting momentarily to disengage his arm from Eddie's and pull his cap down on his head. They disappear, and Thurley turns slowly back towards the *Empire Arms*.)

An uneasy sense of foreboding made him shudder as the reality of that evening slipped away again into its limbo. Thurley felt the damp glass in his fingers; he stared down at the wet ring it left on the marble. He knew Eddie was coming home soon because Brother had told him. Of course Brother had found Thurley another time back in their own city. Brother was down on his luck and finding the good doctor was a windfall. He almost lived at the professor's house after Eddie had gone away, leaving only on mysterious two or three day jaunts, but always like a cat, there on the doorstep one morning when Thurley cracked the door to gather in his milk.

When they talked, it was about Eddie. His face and the throbbing anger visible in his blood wouldn't leave Thurley's mind. It was a thin face, almost like a skull; eyes had glowered at him from pits dug above the cheekbones.

The old woman lay gazing up at the ceiling. Nothing stirred for the room's one window was shut and the hall door had been locked since the night before. It was dark in the room, dark and close with a faint smell of old rags and dry crumbling plaster. Martha's head lay propped on a pillow, slightly inclining towards one side, towards an invisible shoulder somewhere beneath the bedclothes. Although she was alone she frowned, a sullen, tight-lipped frown, and her brown eyes smouldered as if she was scrupulously ignoring someone in the sombre room.

Morning had come, Easter morning, yellow through a nick in the thick green blind but received no recognition from her. It meant only that Bette would soon be at the door asking in her meek, tentative whine, if Mama was O.K., and could she get Mama anything, and are you ready to get up. It meant the room would soon be flooded by yellow light, that she must begin to stir the barely perceptible bulge beneath the covers that was her body. Some mornings she had to scream. Had to drive that whining voice from the door. —Mama are you all right this morning? Voice so full of tenderness, love, hoping against hope there would be no answer. The key would turn slowly in the lock. They would burst in singing and shouting. Throw the blankets back and laugh at her wasted old woman's body. They would rake Gene's shaving things from the dressing table, throw out the old shoes locked in the cupboard. That was all she had. Shoes of her dead lovers. What they had sweated and bled in. Eugene . . . Eugene! Come here boy. Why don't you put these things away like I tell you. You'll have the whole house smelling like a gym. Look, look here everybody what I found. Two dead skunks. Wonder how they got in the house. Bet your brother Eugene brought 'em in his pockets. Boy, get these barges outa this house. I want you to wash 'em tomorrow. I don't care how many games you have to play. And if they're wet you better not put 'em on your feet and wear 'em outa this house. You need to stay home some time anyway. Your brother Edward isn't out running like a wild Indian everyday, and he still manages to live. Stop that pouting now. You look like a big baboon standing there with your lips poked out. Don't start that either cause I ain't feeling sorry for you, no you'll get no sympathy from me so just get 'em out of here, just get 'em out of here, just get 'em out . . .

—Get out, don't you hear, get out . . . I'm not dead yet.

—But Mama, Mama, Eddie's here.

—Eddie?

—Yes Mama, Eddie's back, he's downstairs, just got out of a

cab. Oh you should see him Mama. He looks so good. So straight and tall. Hurry Mama, please get dressed, you know how much he wants to see you.

—Eddie . . . come back. The woman grappled with her confusion; hazy, shifting levels of reality refused to form one distinct world which she could enter. Don't just stand there you fool, open the door, come in and help me. You know I'm a cripple and can't do for myself.

The blind shot up. Before the old woman could raise herself or protest she heard footsteps bounding up the stairs. Her daughter was helping her; between them the pillows were set and her back raised into a half sitting position. She stared into the open doorway still blinking from the sudden burst of light. Over her shoulders long gray-brown braids hung down like little girls'. The dingy flannel nightdress had come open at the throat, and as she slowly twisted, for an instant the sun highlighted the hollow and curve of her neck making the skin soft and smooth again. Through the doorway her lover would return; she bit her lip to make it stop trembling, to assume a smile or frown because Eddie was home.

His head dropped on her bony shoulder. For a moment her arms went around him, feeling only warmth, the hard male back. Hiding her own face, she felt her features scrunch into the wrinkled monkey mask with its years etched so deeply she could read each line. But tears, squandered too long, then dammed longer would not fall. Her voice was breaking, but gruff as she pushed him away.

—You're trying to crush me for sure with that big head of yours. Looking at him, into *her* eyes, seeing the sun gleam on *her* brow still smooth drew the tears dangerously close again. You been gone a while haven't you son? Are you better?

—Yes, Mama, I'm better.

Her eyes were hard, even cold as she listened to his answer. Almost like looking through him, they shifted, searching for

54

some sign, for an indication of truth beyond his voice. His hands, his nose, the open-necked shirt and tee shirt peeking through. Like him long ago after a bath. Standing nude and shivering at inspection, and her voice, are you clean? Ears, armpits, nostrils, between your legs?

—It's good to be home for Easter, Mama. She shifted in the bed, her light body like a leaf rustling.

—You can see I ain't ready for you yet, Eddie. You go on back downstairs and let your sister make me decent. Least as decent as I can get after all these years. You go down and wait in the living room.

—Sure Mama, sure I understand. But you're beautiful Mama, still beautiful like a young girl. He reached out to touch her cheek. She watched the hand float towards her, the long fingers shaping themselves to the contours of her face as it came closer. She drew back, and it dropped, the shape disintegrating, fingers limp, motionless on the purple spread.

—None of your foolishness. I won't have you telling lies the first minute you're back. Now go on downstairs boy. Bette, get my things, and shut that blind, you trying to burn out my eyes?

—Hurry, Mama, please. *Her* eyes in his pleading face looked down at her. Full, moist, deeply set beneath his eggshell brow. She heard him go slowly down the stairs. Almost tiptoeing, as if afraid to waken someone. Now he's quiet, now instead of before when his crippled mother might have been sleeping. Bursting in here, full of nonsense, of old, worn out lies that make me sick to hear 'em. Lies, lies, lies. I'm all right Mama, and I know good and well in a week he'll be with them hoodlums again. Ain't I seen it before. Didn't his father have the same lies. That Brother and the rest of 'em. Always so polite, always so nice. Hello Mrs. Lawson. How are you today Mrs. Lawson. Hope you'll be feeling better soon. And why, just so they can come here for Eddie, and for her, for her too. As if I didn't know. A whore. I don't know how many. Even that ape Brother probably, grinning all the time in Eddie's face. They must all think I'm blind. Well, I'm crippled but not crazy. Nothing wrong with these eyes.

—Bette, shut that blind.

—I did, Mama, it's almost closed.

—Well close it all the way. I'm gonna keep these eyes girl. They still work fine even if the rest of me is dead, and don't you forget it.

The two men sat silently in the small living room. Eddie slightly flushed on the sagging cushions of a sway backed sofa with springs just noticeable beneath the skirts of its rose-flung cover. Brother fidgeted nervously in a straight backed wooden chair. Outside on the back porch a puppy yelped; there were thuds, bumps and a scratching sound as it flung its body, wildly straining at its leash, driven almost mad by a stranger inside the house.

—Do you know what they call it, Brother?

—Teddy.

—Just like the old dog.

—Yeah, Bette said that was what your Mama wanted to call it. Mrs. Lawson sure loved old Teddy.

—What a fat old bitch that dog got to be. Dragged her belly along the ground. And always fighting. Last time I saw her she had her eye half torn out.

—That's the way she died. That big old sore still raw and ugly when they found her. You'd think an old dog would know how to stay outa the way of automobiles.

—Maybe she was just tired. Besides, Bruv, we're getting old and look at us, we aren't any smarter are we? Brother replied with a half smile, then turned his head to gaze through a window. No traffic on the gray asphalt. Dumferline Street. Beyond, the ground rose steeply towards the railroad bed. Spring weeds filled the hillside, shades of green and gray with sudden flecks of tiny white flowers and goldenrods nodding higher up the

56

slope. In fall it was brown. Stiff, dry stalks the color of ancient parchment. Like needles as Eddie remembered through the window, slowly swaying or loud and brittle when he marched through, snapping them down, clusters of dead flowers that disintegrated at his touch. They rattled, shaking themselves free of some last crumbling seed pod, a colorless leaf or stem. With broken arms or necks they leaned earthward as Eddie tromping through delivered a *coup de grâce* with his manlevelling club. Snow would come and then flying down the hardpacked path on sleds or garbage can lids or just plopping butt or belly down and down, down the slope. Coming home damp, numb, shivering at the oven and her angry voice and blows across his shoulders. Get outa those wet things. Is paying doctor bills all I have to do for you brats? Look at these jackets. Ruined, just ruined. That's it, and this time I mean it. You're not stepping outside till the last snowflake is cleaned off that hill. Just look what you've done to my floors. And always tears, ours, hers, and the next day down, down, down again. Some days, summer or spring days, hiking along the tracks on the hillside. Close as we could get to the country. Filled with grasshoppers and flowers, even trees that blossomed and sometimes bore sour cherries or tough green apples. Just walking. Stopping when we wanted to wave at a train or chase some sound in the high weeds or just climb a tree to see where we'd been and where we were going. The tracks ran past a ball field. Just before, we had to cross a forbidden trestle over a busy street then a straight stretch of tracks high above the field and factories. In a vacant lot between the ball field and McKutcheon Brothers was the Bums' Forest. Profuse with trees and weeds growing in the shells of ruined warehouses. Flat stones ranged in circles, ashpiles, tins, grass pressed smoothly in man-size depressions away from the bare trail, and everywhere glass strewn on the ground. In some places layer after layer deep into the earth of broken glass in a hundred shapes and colors. We always stopped to stone from our perch any whole or only partially ravaged bottles. Sometimes the crash of rocks bright against the littered glass would bring angry shouts, even a bleary eyed derelict cursing or threatening to chase us. Once a black bearded old man in a thick army overcoat pelted us in return, stamping his foot and bellowing as his missiles went awry, futilely bounding into the fields, yards away as we made faces and laughed. In the daylight we would sometimes explore the forest. Unexpected bits and pieces would turn up. But at night when we were allowed to go to a ball game, it was always run, run as fast as possible through the trees and shattered walls, hearing the glass crunch like bones under our feet as we dashed towards the smoking lights of the baseball field. But even as we dashed, Eugene, Brother and I with hearts pounding, I remember hearing them sing, somewhere out of sight, the strange, husky singing of winos.

—Brother, do you remember, a long time ago, that old bum throwing stones at us? Brother stopped wringing his hands, and when his face turned from the window, he was grinning.

—Sure man, I remember that old fool, I told you and Gene we oughta wasted him. Remember how you made me stop after I almost knocked his big head off with one of them stones from the tracks? Boy did those babies sail. I coulda killed the old punk, him standing there tossing rocks like a blind man. Half them boulders he threw he could hardly lift.

At the first tap on the stairs Brother's face changed. The red, albino eyes darted around the room, and he shrunk into himself as if he could disappear beneath his cap peak pointing down and his tightly pressed knees pointing up.

—I think I better go, Eddie. Mrs. Lawson don't like me round here. I understand and everything, so don't you feel bad, but I just better go. He was leaning towards his friend, every joint of his angular body forming a tight V. A stick man and only the tip of his buttocks on the wooden chair's hard front.

—Don't talk silly, Bruv. Of course you're welcome here. This is my house too, and Bette's.

Brother's voice was low, almost a groan. —But I wanna go, Eddie. From the porch the dog's yelps were still furious, but becoming hoarse, and his paws scraped less against the wood. On the hillside the goldenrods stirred, glorious as the sun shone. Cars had begun to pass intermittently up and down Dumferline Street. Eddie thought that if he learned to count the methodical tap-shuffle sequences on the stairs, he could always tell how close she had come and how far she had to go. He rose and went into the hall, patting Brother's shoulder as he passed his chair.

—Someday I'm going to kill that pup. Someday I'm going to strangle him with the end of his leash. He won't shut up till we bring the fool in. Eddie can help me, girl, you let him in. Mother and son faced each other in the dark hall.

—Brother's here, Mama. He met me at the station.

—Brother Small! Eddie felt her thin arm stiffen as he half guided, half supported her into the room. Haven't wasted any time have you? Like you didn't have none of your own to meet you. Didn't tell us a thing, but made sure he knew. Wonder she isn't here too.

—Mama! I knew Bette couldn't come, that she had to be here with you. And if I had let you know I was on my way, you would have worried the whole time. Besides, I just wanted to surprise you. I promised last letter it would be by Easter. And that's today, Mama. I wanted to surprise . . .

—I'm too old for surprises, just like I'm too old for lies. You go sit down now where you were and stop hovering over me like some mother hen. The back screen door slammed behind the dog as he bolted through. His paws raked across the linoleum as he bounded, twisting round in circles, falling and rushing, stopping and starting all at once. One last swirling curvet, rearing and up and down like a tiny horse and he dashed towards the old woman's chair, ears back, tongue lolling, his tail busy as a windshield wiper. Disregarding the stranger he nuzzled his dappled rust body against her soft chair, his heaving belly and one forepaw stretched along her steel braces.

—Get down, fool! Where's my newspaper. There was a howl as the pup bounced back from a swift downward blow. He shied away, then slunk out of range, tail between legs, as the old woman brandished a long, hard roll of newspaper, ragged at the edges and frayed along its seam. It sniffed Brother, then Eddie tentatively, still dragging its tail, one eye always on the rolled newspaper which slowly the old woman lowered. No one spoke and in a moment the pup was gaily nuzzling into Eddie's lap.

—The little fool. Eddie watched his mother's face. Her hair was up now, severely pulled back from her high forehead. She seemed owlish and shrivelled, the old-fashioned, steel rimmed glasses covering so much of her face, the bridge pinching her straight nose, the lenses like blank, indifferent moons over the thin line of her set lips.

—He's just a pup, Mama. You shouldn't be so hard.

—You know all about that don't you, Miss. About being young and wild and hard headed. You know how to look for pity too, don't you? I made many mistakes, and all of them because I wasn't hard enough. I'll make more if I live another day, but they won't be for the same reason. Edward, do your friends always keep their hats on in the house?

—I'm sorry Mrs. Lawson. But you know how I am. With a head like mine sometimes people get offended if I take my cap off. I just stopped long ago taking it off altogether except when I sleep or it gets knocked off ever since I gave up the hope of growing hair.

—She knows, Bruv. C'mon Mama. You know how Brother is. Don't make him feel bad. It isn't a sign of disrespect, we all know that. And you never minded before.

—This ain't before, young man. And it is a sorry sight to see *my son* in *my house* putting his voice over mine. But I'm an old sick woman, there's nothing for me to do but sit still and listen. At least I won't have to listen for long. There was a day when I thought I'd always have a man's voice, be it husband's or son's to take my part. But now . . .

60

—Stoppit! You know you don't mean what you're saying. You're just upset this morning, and it's probably my fault for bringing on too much, surprising you like this. Now you have some coffee, Bette, get Mama some coffee please, and me and Brother are going for a walk. It'll give your nerves a chance to settle and let me stretch my legs. We'll both feel better. C'mon, Bruv, let's go walk up by the tracks, it's a bright day and the rails will be shining.

—Good-bye, Mrs. Lawson. I know you're glad to see Eddie. I'll be seeing you some other time. He dawdled behind awkwardly in the doorway, turning his cap over and over in his hands. His horsy features, the pink irises of his albino eyes, the pimples, the lisp as he formed his words doubled and trebled their ugliness. The need to touch, to express what he felt, just to hold another still rather than send him reeling back from the milky ugliness held Brother fixed in the doorway. His lower lip hung, his eyes were glazed over with a thin, opaque membrane. Only the puppy shooting after Eddie as he cracked the outer door roused Brother from himself, made him stoop and catch the rust and white spotted animal to turn it back. Its tongue dabbled wetly against his hands, short, playful barks broke the stillness. Brother shoved against the heaving sides and furiously wagging buttocks, overturning the supple body as it flopped into the middle of the room. As the door slammed he heard its simpers and whimpers, its scratching on the door and Mrs. Lawson's angry voice repeating, —Fool, fool, fool.

—You still tired, Eddie? Eddie didn't answer immediately, intent on the sound of their feet crunching in the gravel along the track bed.

—Nothing so lonely as a long stretch of empty tracks. They came together and disappeared off in the distance, almost incandescent, steel polished to a silver gleam by countless wheels reflecting the sun. At the end of the long level stretch, the atmosphere seemed to dance, like a patch of light seen through a

61

flame, wiggling, rising and falling the steel rails merged with a sunspot. Warm and dry now, dust coating his shoes, Eddie thought of rain, of small closed spaces choking him.

—You feel like going as far as the ball park?

—Sure man, as long as you ain't tired. They trudged watching the sun play off the tracks. It was not quite afternoon but the sun seemed very high. It was still spring heat, benign and life bringing, not the sun that sapped and parched, not the sun that was for Eddie the symbol of endless adolescent afternoons groping in a heavy, blinding light.

—Mama looks just about the same, and she doesn't seem to walk any better. If only we could get her interested in something. Just get her to go outside, try to walk up the street. He talked to himself, not looking at the other man who answered anyway.

—Bette gets her on the porch sometimes. It's just been getting warm enough, but I've seen her a couple times already. Brother kept one hand full of rocks, ricocheting the gray stones off the rails with the other. They struck with a loud clatter, sometimes raising a spark, sometimes just bouncing in lower and lower arcs across the tracks. The weeds in the field below were almost waist high. They had been cleared in some places leaving plots of bare earth where cars or trucks were parked. All the trees were gone. Eddie wanted to say something. He knew Brother was hurt, but there was no answer to the vicious ringing of stone on steel that resonated in the air.

Below, the Bows' sprawling shack still stood, the only house on its side of Dumferline. Its weather-beaten boards were lousy with soot, heavy black coal dust that had settled in clouds over the field, when the old steam engines coughed and puffed. None left. Only the clean diesels like bullets cleaving the air. Across the gleaming rails a tall orange crane, regardless of the holiday, slid on an invisible track along the skyline. When it stopped, a long boom arm swung in a lazy arc over the partially constructed factory it fed with huge chunks of concrete and bundles of girders. On delicate strings ponderous vats were gently lowered, lengths of steel clasped in magnetic pincers dangling from cables, bits of straw in a bird's beak. The machine towered over adjacent rooftops; if there had been trees, it would have dwarfed them also. It would brood over the skeletal frame through the night after all human activity had ceased, its stillness in the moonlight never detracting from the animal life it assumed during the day. In fact it seemed more alive because it slept. Eddie wondered if it would be visible from his window, if its gaunt profile like a crooked cross could be seen at night in the haze of flashing industrial neons. FERGUSON'S BLDG. SUPPLY CO.——MC LEOD'S——KRAUSS AND LEECH INC.——STALLEY'S. What new name would blaze on this building? They had glowered beneath a rose, lime and cobalt blue haze on sleepless nights as he gazed through the window beside his bed. Then a train roaring, rattling as if dropped from a great height down on the tracks then just as swiftly swept up again. The old engines whistled, sometimes they left thin trails of white smoke, floating luminous in the darkness. On one one day. On one one day—on one one day—on one one day churned by the wheels.

—Whatever happened to Henry Bow? Brother's forehead creased, he tossed one more stone high and far towards the sun. He remembered Eddie fighting Henry Bow beneath the water tank. Henry had whopped him good and I had to just stand and watch cause Henry could whop us both at the same time if he wanted and two on one wasn't fair anyway. That Eddie sure has some funny bags, even when he was a kid fighting Big Henry Bow like that just cause he said something, just cause he put Mrs. Lawson in the dozens, but Eugene whopped Henry later cause I squealed, then Henry whopped me one day, taking my cap too cause he found out I squealed, in the alley with nobody watching, him on top whopping shit outa me till he got tired. Sure I cried. I wasn't no sissy, but hell it was easier screamin' from the first rather than being like Eddie and trying to fight gettin' in a few licks that just made Henry madder and coming like a bull or ape or some black ugly animal taking little, skinny Eddie apart. Took my cap too, the one I liked and he knew, so he peed on it the black bastard, peed on it and buried it somewhere on the hillside. I could have killed him but better just to start crying and take low than getting him madder and I ain't got no big brother to whip Henry and keep him off, just Alice, just Alice who Eddie always liked and I knew and she liked him but scared and fighting each other always instead. What's Eddie asking now. Henry Bow I remember him, that old shack down there that's what made Eddie think but after all these years and he ain't never mentioned before that name Henry Bow, yes I remember all about Henry Bow with that crazy daddy of his that shot them robbers, Shootemup was what he was called, Sam Shootemup after they came to rob him Sunday cause he sold liquor and wasn't supposed to that day so he had lots of bread that day and they came sneaking down out the weeds two cats thought they could scare the old man, and that he couldn't tell the cops for being afraid they'd take him for selling booze anyway on the Lord's day so down they snuck and like I heard it, he saw them and when they comes in the back door, all the old wood creaking he would of heard them anyway less they waited for a train, a long noisy freight, so there he was just sitting behind the counter all that bread and booze right there but he was waiting and they got nothing but a blast of buckshot and as I heard it told he said I'll give you bastards five to drop them icepicks and get your asses off my property fast as you can go cause I'm going to give one barrel then another straight up your buttholes then Sam laughed and started counting one-two-three and you never seen niggers hauling butt so quick—wham—wham that buckshot spreading out and smoke and niggers screaming he said two punks I never seen before but ugly, boy was they ugly, a yellow one and a big black but both lost all their color looking down that fat mouthed shotgun and lickety-split off they went so I heard Mister Bow tell it and ever since Shootemup's they called it where you used to be able to get booze on the Lord's day.

—Sellin' bootleg whiskey somewhere I bet, just like his old man.

—I can just see that big bully pushing rotten booze. Did you ever notice, Brother, how his hands were always black, and the back of his neck, and shirts? Lot of guys sweat, everybody sweats, but Henry sweat black coal dust. I never forgot the dirty words coming out of his mouth and that look he gave me, like he just knew a skinny runt like me would have to take it or at best go tell my big brother like I was a girl or something that had to run home for help.

—You still was crazy, man. Henry was just too big. You shoulda run off and bricked 'em. I'd have helped you. We'd have killed that big punk, or at least taught him to leave us alone. Just cause his old man shot some hard-up niggers.

—Those dirty fists coming down on me. It was like slow motion. I saw him raise each one, then watched it falling closer and closer. After a while it was like watching fireworks, shooting up, bursting then trailing sparks back down to earth somewhere far away. I didn't even feel it after a while. Just the dirty fist up flashing then down like rain.

—Gene whopped his big ass good when he caught 'em.

—You shouldn't have told, Brother. I had finished with Henry. It was enough; it was over. That time I didn't need Gene to help.

—Sometimes I wish I hadn't. But that's cause of what he did to me over in Carter's Alley. I wish Gene woulda whopped him after that. I remember thinking down there on my back with him whalin' me I had already had my laugh and he was gettin' his last and I wouldn't get no more.

They were standing above the Bums' Forest. Brother knelt to tie his shoe. A train was rushing up the tracks behind them. It was only a tiny red box down the silver threads, but already the rails had begun to sing. Brother turned to watch it grow, to feel terror as it rapidly increased in size and intensity, its roar louder and louder, its form attenuating, growing sharp and distinct like a blunt shark's head with a grim chrome smile. Something aimed at him, headlong, bleating as it rushed across the trestle, some beast shrieking, thundering that for a moment would take him trembling into its entrails. He shook as the train rumbled past, part of its roar, its speed, vibrating in time to its tremendous surging. rhythm, a rate his human frame could endure only an instant.

For Eddie it came like a black cloud, shutting out everything—the stunted trees, the weeds and bushes just springing into green life, the dilapidated foundations and brilliant plots of glass embedded in the earth. He was plunged as he looked into night, into chill autumn, a leaf falling night when a fire burned red and yellow under a close, black, starless sky and winos were singing.

Why me here searching? Why not Eugene, who is bigger and not afraid and who is loved? Why do they sing? Why do they drink and break the bottles and scatter glass here where they must sleep? And the other things they do, here where they must sleep. Why? Surely they smell it too. And why so close and yet none of them can I see? Their singing, why is it like nothing else? Not boys or girls, men or women. Not like the choir at our church or Mama when she sings or what I've heard on the radio. Like nothing, but some of everything. If I sing too, will I be less afraid? Will they call me to come join them around the fire over there behind that wall? Should I call him? Daddy, Daddy, Daddy. And if they call should I go? What if the old one in the army coat . . . why did he try to lift such huge ones? If him there and me close a huge one dropped on my head, crushing, mashing me down like the bottles, in pieces mashing me down. Daddy, Daddy. Why me searching these dark woods? Surely Eugene better, he loves Eugene. Where is Brother? Brother would come with me, he loves. These deep

66

woods. Pee smell and piles like dogs only bigger, and I know it's not dogs. Wine smell and sick smell, pools of it slicking the grass or dried on stones and the glass. I feel glass through my shoes, jagged, sharp, cutting edges. Pressing always up and through. Why does it hate, why does it thrust its sharp nose into my feet? They would know me here. All the ones we've stoned. Jumping like cats from the grasses, shouting things at us. In that big army coat. Like squirrels springing out, chattering. Smash, smash. Daddy, Daddy. Mama wants you home. Please come Daddy, please come.

It was gone, and suddenly again the sun shone warm on his back. How deep and cool a shadow can be. How deep so you can walk miles in a small one and be so tired so quickly. The train seemed to suck away all the air. Eddie breathed deeply after it passed, glancing over his shoulder where Brother and the shadow had been.

On one one day . . . on one one day . . . on one one day . . . on one one day. The orange crane was still. Easter only a half day, the ants had descended from the skeleton. Beyond, the neon tubing was gray and lifeless, the names barely readable if Eddie hadn't known them so well. On one one day . . . on one one day.

—Hey Bruv, what you thinking about, man? You're like a statue standing there. You think if you pose long enough someone will take your picture?

—Just thinking man. Sometimes I do you know. Things make me think more than people—things like trains. People's confusing, can't do nothing but think what they said or what they're doing and forget most of that, but things is different. I can think about a train. Trains is always trains.

—Or a cap?

—Yeah, Eddie, you know what I mean. He patted the cap on his head smiling. And I can think about you too, Eddie, I can think about you. He lifted his cap, slowly mopping a ring of sweat from his bare head with a gray wad of handkerchief pulled from his hip pocket. Eddie watched as the sun glinted from Brother's hairless dome, his albino ugliness the sun lit so profusely.

—I'm going home now. Capped again Brother nodded in reply still squinting from the sun in his eyes. As Eddie tromped along between the gravel bed and the high swaying grasses, Dumferline Street seemed far away. A million miles beyond the tops of weeds stirred by a weak breeze. It seemed a shame the trees should have gone. Those few scraggly fruit trees and the one or two others he didn't know the names of. After that certainly the rest too. It was funny to think of himself, hiding out there in the weeds. Had snow ever been there? Behind him he heard stones smacking against the tracks.

The Buick rolled steadily along. Thurley didn't drive fast, but he had style behind the wheel; he gave the impression that he had been driving big, dark limousines all his life. It was a borrowed car. From his more than comfortable income Thurley had never been able to save enough at one time to afford the down payments on a new one. Always something else first, a trip to Europe, an antique, books, gin. For a moment he thought of smiling Hermann. What kind of car did he drive?

The weatherman had been wrong. *Mild showers may daunt the less hardy marchers in today's Easter parade.* Such a smiling voice, with overtones and undertones of the deadliest sincerity. *A high pressure front blown down from Canada will collide with the lingering warm front that has brought us such sunny blue skies. All the Eastern seaboard is threatened with shower activity.* Rain, rain go away Little Bobbie wants to play. He mashed the accelerator, dipping out and around an old Ford, straddling the broken white line as a burst of power shot the Buick forward. Handles like a roadster. Cruising now, a long empty stretch before him. Thurley lit himself a cigarette from the open pack laying on the padded dash. Everything worked. Lighter, horns, wipers, automatic windows, air conditioning, radio, even the square faced clock with Roman numerals. It was like Noonan, big, efficient, a world all to itself gliding along perfectly performing its functions. *Impermeable.* Everything Thurley wasn't. In a flurry, he pushed every button, turned every knob, the car tooted, heated, windows eerily rose up and down around him, music blared, the windshield was squirted and wiped, an aerial climbed then shrunk within itself. Like a child I am he thought, fascinated because the world was once again at his fingertips. Thurley relaxed as he smoked; the car relaxed and sped quietly down the tree lined highway.

Two-forty-five. He would be there before three-thirty. That left time for a few drinks with Al before they went to the chapel. It was a good idea, something that for once he was really glad he had thought of. An Orthodox Easter service. Music and pageantry, what he knew he couldn't resist. Something stuck deeply into the past, something that would reward the intense participant with a giddy headlong flight backwards through time, along one of those fine, vital skeins that like interminable veins feed the present, making it more than madness, making him more than an occasional partaker of its insanity. He had invested so much of himself in finding these paths, in following the mysterious lines as they sunk into obscurity, into the abyss of time. Somewhere, all he could visualize was a cold, brilliant valley glazed with a light crust of snow, all lines converged. The past in one bold epiphany would manifest itself as an answer. Perhaps a footprint in the immaculate snow, or a throne dazzling across the frozen depression. These were his own fancies. He believed that if he proceeded far enough there would be a man, a beautiful, soft-spoken man whose eyes were acquainted with grief, who knew sorrow and had experienced grace, who would welcome him with a hand round his shoulders saying simple things, pure, simple things that exhausted all further inquiry, all disquiet, final, truthful things as they glided

69

back and forth through immense silences. Thurley dreamed of an eternity of these walks beside the soft-spoken stranger. The books he read, and the words he wrote were preparation.

Did he believe? The books, the countless manuscripts yellowing somewhere, each the humble seercloth of some proud beginning. Why do you do it, why do you bother then? Sometimes in the middle of the night the persistency of this question as he lay fully awake and keenly conscious was more horrible than the most elemental nightmare. He had no devils to fear. Once, an edge of his imagination bordered a realm of monsters and devils. It was perdition's scourging pit, the Baptist hell of his father and mother. He had still trembled reading the *Portrait*'s description of hell as a college freshman at Harvard. He was embarrassed and ashamed, never mentioned it to anyone, but still trembled when alone at the hell of his fathers. But that was all past, the devils had become ridiculous or benign, like gargoyles who grimaced and leered from medieval chapels. He was no longer superstitious, but how different was blind superstition from his harrowing disbelief in the mechanical, everyday activities of his life? That overriding doubt and scepticism sapping the vital fluid from his life which he brooded on just as surely as an ascetic priest on sin. Was it conscience?

He swerved to avoid something dead on the roadside. Was it conscience, simply the old religious fear disguised out of recognition to something less unreasonable, less barbaric and shameful? *The agenbite of inwit*. He smiled, letting the quotation drain off the building intensity. *Quotation is as close to reality as they can get*. Was it Stendhal, or was it some aside in the Rostovs' glittering salon? Perhaps even Flaubert. Sounds like a conclusion he would come to after leafing through his trunk of *idées reçus*. A buffer zone now. Peaceful, easy bumps in the limbo of other minds. No sharp edges here. No inbites. Did he seek it on purpose? Did he stock his mind against these threatening moments? Not a cloud in the sky. Do I believe? They must know what they're talking about. Weathermen are scientists aren't they? Conclusions only from facts. Their data resting on reality. Not like us, not the wily humanist playing with the clay of his own utterly malleable, therefore utterly deceptive and unreliable being. I started with a question. I have rallied round me other minds, other words. I am filled to overflowing with parentheses, with qualifications, with ambiguity and paradox. And what have I become, what has become of the question posed? It is armoured, it is inviolable. Hung up by the multifariousness of the *me*. The whine of self-consciousness like Bartholemew's hats that can't be removed. *How shall I presume?* London? Rome? Athens? New York? Cambridge? I have posed a question. Surely it is presumption to suppose I may pose. The inkling of fear. The high fence of hubris stalling our progress. Do I dare, do I dare? How poignant the cross. The seven words. What did he really say? And were they not questions of the highest order? Lost, lost, forsaken is the only answer. To pose an inviolable question. The pride we have in the untampered, the stark, resounding question that refuses to be tainted by an answer. The fierce oscillation ringing between null and void that destroys our souls. And if I pose it, intensely, in a posture of supplication it is enough. I am done, finished, complete. Is it conscience?

I am placated by a weather report. Oh what lovely trees. Serried ranks, a skirt of sunlight beneath, translucent, girding the bare bottoms. How I would love to face the truth, just for a moment, even to be blinded on the tenth step and pitch backwards even into a lake of fire. What could be worse than this machine? Enclosed in its steel guts, propelled by explosions I can't feel the heat of or see the fire. Sometimes it's like looking over a battlefield. Everything dead, stinking to heaven, my task at best to loot the dead, finish the dying.

Of course I believe. How crystal clear it is. I have converted, seen the light, my salvation on the solid rock of the Church. Chartres in the moonlight, its exterior lace. Its towers two unshakable ramparts. The beads, the Hail Marys, the lucid, picturesque ritual. All there in black and white. How many angels on a pinhead? The fierce soldiers of Christ, Loyola's standard cracking like a whip. Cardinal Guevara in his chair. Something strange about the perspective. Like awkward medieval painting, Cimabue, Cavallini, planes of reality distorted or ignored, the Cardinal almost dumped from his chair into the profane living-room. A son of the Church. After so long returning to the bosom. How she would turn over in her grave, her Baptist grave in the family plot. There's always been a Thurley. Dates barely readable on the oldest stones. Magnolias, mimosas languid over-head. The grass and dainty flowers sprinkled through it. It wasn't the veranda any more without her sitting rocking. It curved around the big white house. Flat, slightly sloping from the walls towards the spacious lawn, a wooden railing with carved white posts like attenuated urns, posts that were loose and wobbly at certain spots from being leaned on, sat on or climbed over by generations of Thurleys. How many mint juleps consumed in its shade, how many hours logged in the gliders, sofa, chairs and rockers ranged on their appropriate woven mats. Thurley was there, more easily than he thought possible, out of the speeding Buick and home again, home again.

—Bobbie, Bobbie, look at those knees. He jerked up, im-mediately standing at attention in his bright sailor suit. The blue shorts had ridden up his chubby thighs and his blue socks had rolled down to coils around his ankles.

—Look at you Robert Thurley. We're never going to make a gentleman out of you. His fat cheeks blushed, timidly he raised his ruddy arm adjusting the white collar and matching cap. Now you get in there right away and tell Hattie I said to wash those knees and tidy you up. My, my, if I hadn't known you were mine, I'd think you were one of those little niggerboys from down the road with that dirty face and those knees. In there right now Master Robert.

He marched up the long white steps, and into the house call-ing for Hattie. She came, the model for Aunt Jemima Thurley always thought of her later, bustling and black with that half anxious, half smiling moon of a face peering down at him, always going straight to the root of whatever he was feeling.

—I heard your Mama scolding, Master Robert.

—I didn't do nothing, Hattie, I was just playing. He was on her knee, the strange powder, sweat, clean calico aroma settling around him like a cloud. She was soft too like a cloud, like jelly as he squirmed but really didn't mind the hands and the cloth rubbing his dusty legs.

—What was you playing, Master Robert, coal miner? She smiled down at him, the big moon sinking, showing little eyes that twinkled and teeth. He giggled back. The cloth tickled; her pillowy boobies when he leaned back bounced unsupported beneath the bright calico.

—Sit still li'l mister. Where you trying to get to? He wiggled and laughed outright now, beating a tattoo with the insides of his bare knees against her fat thighs.

—Hey, hey, hey you little rascal, I ain't no rocking horse. He leaped down running out of the kitchen through the long, high hall prancing as he ran trailing the floppy white collar still on a cloud.

Thurley slowed down for a turning, fascinated by the clicking sound as he blinked his signal. Everything automatic. It was actually ages since he'd driven. Always taxi cabs. Taxi cabs like hotel rooms that sometimes gave him that sick, lost sensation in the pit of his stomach. This outing had come to him like a storm. Why not? Haven't seen Al in ages, Easter's a holiday, and the special service was supposedly spectacular, well worth the trip in itself. He didn't need these reasons at all. He had the idea and decided all at once. A positive idea. That alone was startling, exhilarating. But as he came closer, he had to admit it was to Al that he was making his pilgrimage. Not so much spontaneous, but the inevitable climax of a slow subtle process. How often had he thought of Al? At the strangest times, and in a variety of totally disassociated situations over the past few years Al had incongruously popped up, and because he had been involved in other things at these moments, disappeared without allowing Thurley any time to elaborate on his sudden presence. Probably some sort of defense mechanism Thurley thought, to release pressures Al symbolized. Like a dream . . . probably a name for the Freudian paradigm, a word that would explain it, would explain Al . . . a little psychology a dangerous thing . . . dispose of Al. I don't even want to do that, that's not it at all . . .

Just a few more miles, a matter of minutes. Al's cloister. Had he found peace? Teaching music here on a quiet campus. Would that dispose of Al? Thurley drove slowly, cautiously now, repeating to himself the directions he had memorized, watching for road signs, landmarks. *A big Dairy Queen on the corner. Two streets then left. Sycamore, left again. Row of big brick houses, well kept lawns and shrubs, mine a white shingle stuck on corner after these.* Funny the details people pick as substantial, as identifying something or themselves. The car seemed to purr now, Thurley half expected it to be sleeked with a light coat of sweat as he climbed out shutting the door with a solid thud behind him. Still sun shining, birds singing *Oh what a lovely Easter day* as he shuffled up the short flagstone path feeling the kinks quietly protesting in his legs. Like flowers, groups of people, mostly families, sizes assorted from Papa Bear to Baby Bear strolled along the broad, grass bordered pavements. Not a cloud in the sky as he knocked.

Al. Al Levine all aflutter, embracing Thurley, pushing him to arm's length, pulling him close again, his hard little hand and arm furiously pumping clasped into the other's. Like a little boy neatly tucked into his three piece suit, Al made happy, indistinguishable sounds as he hustled his friend into the livingroom.

—Something cold right away, right. Just sit down, there, on the sofa. He moved, pointed and talked with a disarmingly fluttery precision, disappearing and returning with a wooden tray holding two tall gin tonics it seemed all in one motion and breath. Like a nerve end twitching, soft, fluttering Al.

—Wonderful Bob, just wonderful, not another ounce or wrinkle since last time. Here's to you. Cheers! Half a frosted glass tumbled down Al's throat. His Adam's apple bobbed, and he spoke again as soon as his throat had cleared. What a day, what a day this is. You sure can pick them. Ha! It took Easter to bring you though, three Easters in fact, this is the third you know. But that makes it lucky doesn't it, at least between a couple of old occultists like us. Easter! Good old Thurley doesn't miss a trick does he, what an upstage, what an upstage. His twangy but distinct pronunciation of each syllable got the most out of words. Talking to Al was always being on the edge of your seat, listening to a verbal flow that reminded Thurley of a tennis game. The words bounding back and forth, and just one player, Al, serving, returning, bing, biff on both sides of the net. That quick side to side movement straining the neck muscles Thurley felt when he listened could only be compared to a spectator on the edge of his chair enthralled, breathless, hoping both that someone would miss and that the words would never stop bounding high and white across the net.

—You're here, Bob, you're here. It's like all those words thawing to life after the long, cold winter in Paul Bunyan. You know that story don't you? Why it's part of the American heritage isn't it? I mean myth, real myth or as close as we've come —Paul Bunyan, Natty Bumppo, Johnny Appleseed, Mike McGraw, old John Henry, no let's not forget John, last but not least breaking his gut driving rails. Cried the first time I heard that story. You know it don't you? The race . . . that nasty machine laying rails behind him. Chug, chug, like a shadow creeping up on poor black John. Pow. His heart broke. Just couldn't be beaten. Just wouldn't lie down, couldn't stop, so Pow. He took another deep drink, swilling the liquid visibly in his throat.

—Bob, Bob, you're here. He stood over Thurley, a gnome, a

pixie in his immaculate Ivy cut suit. Always dapper, always neat and clean. He stood close and silent for a moment as if he knew he was being appraised, posing, paying his respects to Thurley's admiration. Same Al. Small, delicate, below the neck groomed and tailored almost out of existence. Tight and hard. Even the small head sharp and angular seemed somehow like a knot. His hair was thinning but jet black, still long and slick. It looked painted on his skull, and his eyes and the accentual lines of his face seemed limned with the same hue. Sparkling eyes. Coal black, pricked with spots of light. Nothing could be whiter than his cuffs, shirt front and collar.

—I promised myself to be quiet today. To listen for a change. I want to hear about you, Bob, if it's possible, if there are words I want to hear them. After fixing more drinks Al sat quiet and attentive on a donkey saddle stool, the tray between him and his visitor already dyed with circles and half-moons from the sweating glass.

—Funny how it all comes rushing back, all the closeness and understanding like a kick in the pants driving me right to the edge . . . why Bob, why the long silence between us? Like a pit, or a big hole. It's urgent now, Bob. Everything's come back since I heard from you and started to really believe you were coming. And Easter . . . only you could pull that off. Thurley on the third year returning.

Between them the frosted glasses teared. Like tired horses sweating while their riders, invigorated from pushing them half to death, chat coolly in the shade. Al was like a little boy now. His slim legs in tapered Dacron trousers crossed oriental style as he slipped to the floor from the scooped saddle seat. Something from Greece Thurley remembered, brought back by Miriam, Al's wife, how long ago. It was covered with boldly patched quilting, primitive and striking against which Al reclined his neck and narrow unpadded shoulders beneath the open suit jacket. A boy now, exhausted at the end of a day of hiking or ball playing, content to sip his Coke and listen to the tired voice of any old man who would tell him an old story.

—I'm glad we only have a little time, Al. I really don't have much to say. Just the thought of saying anything begins to fatigue me. And besides how many original or entertaining ways are there to say nothing?

—Probably quite a few. And for some you can even earn a living. Thurley traced a pattern in the carpet. Quick gins began to demand their due. He felt a momentary giddiness, then the start of a soft, gradually unfolding languor.

—You remembered how I like my gin and tonic. Al laughed in reply, tilting his delicate head forward, pouting his lips, blinking both eyes several times in an exaggerated expression of *how could I* or *are you kidding*. Thurley smiled back conscious he was thinking his unrelated, private thoughts aloud. He paused, trying to pull the fuzzy pictures together, then went on more consciously, straining for something both natural and reserved, something controlled that would filter and select through the gray mass of his impressions, to give freely but not all. He searched not only for a place to begin, but for a reminiscence of where they had ended, how far they had been accustomed to penetrate each other's skins in that prolonged intimacy of a few years before. Al was an equal, no talking up or down, all words, feelings legitimate. But even here there were fences and no trespassing signs deeply set. What could they share on this Easter afternoon? Ghosts? Even these brought up problems, because nothing ever really dies. Here they were in this room to prove it.

—How are Miriam and Sandra? That was safe enough, the divorced wife, the beautiful child, so sensitive, so wide-eyed, full of love and belief that stroking her soft brown hair was like running his old man's hand over a razor.

—Miriam's fine so I hear. Still at Sarah Lawrence. The kid writes me once a month. Sweetest letters. God, what a beautiful kid.

—And the music? Thurley was repelled by his own crudeness, his stupid, probing tongue as soon as the question dropped. Why that, why mention the only other thing Al cares for in the

77

world after bringing up the picture of his lost daughter? But the question brought a sort of relief to Al's face. His narrow shoulders seemed to broaden, and he sat taller and straighter. His tone was almost coy.

—Surprises, surprises, Bob. He wrung his tiny, smooth hands. Strange how white and smooth the palms, the backs covered with coarse, jet-black hair. Like a monkey from the back. Al's one visible defect, the flaw in his sculptured, immaculate compactness. Easier to make little people perfect. To mold the limbs and the small faces delicately in miniature. But even there slip-ups, something dangling, out of place, or covered with thick, black hair.

—Something new, something big? Thurley let his enthusiasm run away with caution, he clumsily plowed through what might be open wounds if he had inferred incorrectly from Al's elfish reply. But no, Al continued to grin, to act out a boy carrying a hot, delicious secret.

—Later for me, Bob. I'm saying nothing about me till after I've heard you. You're the guest. You've rolled back the stone, arrived here Easter afternoon upstaging the Messiah. Thurley Anesti. I'm just ears till you finish.

Thurley glanced down at his watch. Less than an hour. Al's insistence began to bother him a little. He hadn't come to confess. He knew that now, sitting in the strange room, Al squatting before him. He wanted to ask him to play something. Chopin, Mozart, something sane, clear, exquisitely structured, like the little girl with flying pigtails who used to run through Al's ramshackle cottage in Maine. That little laughing girl with all her bones showing. No secrets there, and yet something that could never be known, not because it hid itself or refused to be discovered, but because her beauty gave of itself more deeply than anyone could ever ask.

—I'm a fool. A blunderer as always, Bob. Please excuse me. I didn't mean to push, to try to turn you on and play you like I would a batch of L.P.s. But you know how it is. So close so long, then nothing—poof. Suddenly three years later I get a card, and a few days after, you come sailing into my living-room. I wanna know something, anything. It's like an ache, I wanna get inside you, or at least if it's been too long, close enough to feel the old warmth. He rose, his slim legs straight-ened, the creases of the miracle fabric obediently falling into place. He paced about the room, short and for Al slow steps, stopping here and there as if he were unfamiliar with his sur-roundings, examining them as if they were new and great im-portance was attached to a correct and thorough appraisal of the room and its objects. He rubbed the back of a puce overstuffed chair, scanned the elegant eighteenth-century bindings tightly packed in glass bookcases, scrutinized each knickknack and souvenir adorning the flat surfaces, moved his feet tentatively through the thick piled rugs scattered on the floor. His longest pause was in front of a large ink drawn nude over the brick fireplace. Her form was outrageously soft and round. Not cur-licued like a Rubens but thick, maternal curves all thigh, hip and bust like a massive Maillol bronze. She was reposing, sub-missive, an odalisque. Cascading to a scruff of wiry hair her stomach protruded like a melon; her eyes were fixed on this curve.

The march around the room said what had to be said, Al was a stranger too. There had been during the interim nothing to displace fear, loneliness and pain, what they had felt before when together, and what was still all that mattered. Down, down tumbling. Each mask topples, the actor bows, but out beyond the blinding lights there is silence, not a sound, not a cough or a grunt. Panicked, another mask is discarded, still nothing, and another, another, another and another. Still the blank, soundless void. Bowing and stripping the actor dies. Still nothing.

—I'll get us another. Al took a long time. Thurley found him-self staring at the naked woman. Her thighs, breasts, the bush like an animal climbing her round belly. Thurley the bride-groom, Eleanor on his arm. They had gone South to the Thurleys' ancestral pile for the wedding. It was all a show, a sad, desperate show, and as folly succeeded folly, drink succeeded drink, until Thurley had felt the accumulated horror like a wild beast in his guts that must be drowned.

Bride and groom stood on the veranda. Behind them through long French windows the sounds of genteel drunkenness and excess lilted. A hired band, mostly violins, played undaunted till the backs and underarms of their thin white coats were dark with sweat. Waltz after sickly waltz. Only once had some old aunt asked for a country dance—the musicians and other relatives grudgingly complied, the company dispersing to line the four walls of the ballroom each face daring the other to submit to the music's jaded syncopation. Thurley drew his bride closer, letting his hand slip low on her waist till he felt the enormous flounce of her thousand crinoline slips beneath the white lace begin. The music stopped. Only muffled voices drifted from behind the tall windows. Thurley could hear crickets and the dry rustle of the thousand slips. Her gown glowed. Not solid and yellow like the lightning bugs blinking out over the lawn, but like a ghost or a white shadow, amorphous, shifting. Other white ghosts glided in the darkness. Couples taking advantage of the intermission to stroll in the balmy night air, to dry sweat under their evening clothes, or just to find a tree or bush. The musicians stood in a white clump apart, lit for a moment in the glare of a match, huddling close as if for warmth from its tiny flame. Red points of burning ash bobbed.

Eleanor was bored and tired. She wanted a cigarette terribly but she would wait, at least till tomorrow maintain the image unblemished. What foolishness. So this is the Old South and I am by proxy a Southern belle. Proud of it too, they are. This big white barn of a house, the liege lord Thurleys and their guests. Honey, this, Honey that. And always my lovely Bobbikins there to cushion the blows, to spoon-feed them to me and me to them. A regular trooper he's been, held up so well all along. Grinning at the bitch who cooed to me. What a lovely girl, she said, my, my, Bobbie, I'm afraid us pore li'l country gals just don't stand a chance if all the Northern ladies are like Miss Eleanor. His arm around me all the time, yea though we walk, fear no evil. His arm squeezing, so tight I can't breathe.

—It's a beautiful night isn't it, dear? Thurley leaned closer to smell her perfume and hair. Couldn't be closer to perfect. He pointed with his cocktail glass, slopping out a silver glob that splattered loudly against the floorboards. That was my world once, Eleanor. Nothing existed beyond these acres of finely nurtured Thurley grass. You can't see very well now, but you must have noticed already how beautiful the grounds really are. Li'l Bobbie's Garden of Eden. But sans apple tree, sans Eve even. I guess it just goes to show. He used a loaded deck. The snake was enough. The itty-bitty worm in the grass. Look at 'em sneaking off to the woods. Back to nature they go. Can you imagine any man putting his hands on those powder puffs? Down here we make real women, soft, affectionate, one hundred per cent fluff balls. Could any man in his right mind believe there's anything under all those buttons and bows, that there's flesh, live warm flesh. He emptied the glass too quickly, gin dribbled on his chin, —ha, my cup runneth over. I'd better be careful, mustn't spoil our nuptial rites, disappoint Hymen. The bridegroom cometh. Wish this thing I thee wed . . .

—Stoppit, Bob. You're drunk. She didn't raise her voice, just said it calmly, professionally, in the almost bored tone of a physician pronouncing death.

—Aw, Baby.

—Take your hand away please, I can barely breathe. She twisted from the circle of his arm, the white dress rustling as she stepped away. It's getting late isn't it, I mean a decent interval has elapsed since the ceremony. Let's get away from here. I've been on display long enough.

—Not yet, Baby, please not yet. I wanna tell you about my garden, about how it used to be before that nasty old man with the sword drove me away.

—You're not being funny, Robert. I'm tired, I just want to go to bed.

—To bed, to sleep, to dream, that's the rub. Never could figure that out exactly, but then it doesn't matter. I mean the whole speech is simply an elaborate question mark. It's not time yet, the night is young and so are we. He grabbed her hand raising it as he slipped his other arm around her waist, trying to coax her stiff body into a waltz. Swaying and humming he wanted to guide her into the flamboyant steps he rehearsed. Tra la tra la. The night's young, Baby.

She pulled forcibly away. —I'm going, Robert. If you don't want to make us both look foolish you'd better come with me.

—In dulcet tones my Aramantha beckons. Trip, trip fantastic toes. Spinning wildly, his whole body fluttered into a solitary dance. Alone on the veranda he spun and spun, oblivious until the French doors were flung open and on a cloud of cheers, jeers, salutations and ribaldries his name floated out.

Hurry up now it's time, hurry up now it's time, hurry up now.
They had been loaned the master bedroom. The others kept him downstairs an hour, pouring drinks down his throat, patting and pulling, tendering innuendos with each handshake, interminably winking and pinching. The wedding party partaking of a foretaste. Protesting mildly Thurley floundered in the mass of friends and family, somehow for a moment resting on his mother's shoulder, her old throat circled in lace, the green pin an eye on her flat chest, so close he wanted to cry, but quickly whisked away, someone pumping his hand, some arm around his shoulder, the soft, pink smell as he was nuzzled, a wet, flacid imprint on his cheek, violins, the crystal layers of chandelier climbing one another.

Hurry up now it's time.
—Where is Eleanor, where is my bride? Staggering, he made his way into the high, long hall, shedding the voices, hands, the bright, dancing lights of the ballroom. Like emerging from the bottom of the ocean, or being stripped naked he thought

alone suddenly in the throes of a valiant effort to maintain his dignity. Look at those knees boy, look at those knees. He would never be a gentleman, never. She must come clean me up. I'll sit still, I promise Hattie, I promise. Who had kissed him, that horrible, horrible kiss. Like death, a drowned woman puckering on my cheek. Never thought it would be wet. Always believed it would be dry, grainy, rasping like sandpaper or a file. There is nothing underneath. Dry, dusty there like old clothes or feathers.

He climbed the broad twisting stairs, slumping at intervals against the graceful banister. When he reached their borrowed bedroom, the light was out and Eleanor lay asleep, a thin sheet covering her nakedness. Like the gown the linen sheet glowed, but incredibly solid, a piece of marble into which had been cut the epitome of female form. All contour, curve and hollow abstracted, into smooth, hard stone. Thurley slowly undressed. As he bent to ease off a patent leather pump from his swollen foot, he was startled by the gown, ghostly white, standing in a corner like another Eleanor. He went to it, for some reason kneeling, pushing his face into the billowing skirts, listening to the slips like cellophane dry crinkling beneath. When he moved away, it toppled in a heap, the sound of silk like a parachute dying. Eleanor did not stir. She had one end of the sheet wrapped under her body and her arm held down the other. Thurley slouched over her, finally naked, perplexed and ridiculous in the moonlight filtering through an open window behind him. He tugged lightly at the crisp, cool material where it stretched tautly on the empty side of the bed. The sheet wouldn't move. At its touch on his bare back he wanted to weep.

—We'd better make it a quick one Bob, not much time before the big show. Al placed a tumbler in his hand. Thurley listened to the ice cubes bumping their glass walls like notes of a miniature xylophone. More than anything he wanted to say his wife's name. He wanted to pronounce *Ele-an-or* clearly and distinctly, nothing more, no story, nothing, just say the word.

But it wasn't just the word, and he couldn't say why he couldn't say it. Words had meaning, something solid to rest on, something which if ambiguous could at least be private and significant. Eleanor. If somehow it could be said in this room, said to Al, it would help so much. Al had a wife. He had lost her, and a daughter too. I said *Miriam* first thing—I asked Al about Miriam. Miriam's a word, Miriam can be mastered even if it's an unpleasant, even a painful task. But my wife, my Eleanor . . .

—Too much tonic in that one? Thurley realized he had been frowning, that Eleanor uninvited sat like a stone in the room.

—No, no it's fine, Al. I'm just a little distracted. It's too much all at once, the two of us alone, drinking together after all this time. Like the wind has blown a door open and it's sucking everything away and I can't close it. Just run round like crazy grabbing at bits and pieces before they're blown away . . . just scraps, pages out of order and half written. Thurley heard the wind, saw the door flapping, the air filled with paper. Somewhere in that snow of fluttering, swirling sheets was one written *Eleanor*.

—Eleanor.

—Whadya say, Bob? Al had been gazing again at the nude. He believed that he had heard correctly, that his friend had said *Eleanor,* but if he was mistaken . . . Excuse, me, I'm daydreaming too now, what was it you said?

—I don't even know myself, muttering, thinking aloud. Thurley concentrated on the second hand idly circling the black face of his watch. *Hurry up now, it's time, hurry up now. Please gentlemen, it's time.*

—What's happened to us, Bob, what's happened? We might as well be a million miles apart.

Was it conscience? Thurley knew some things had not been ironed out, would in no sense ever be finished. The night Al had come into his bed. The three of us, Al, Eleanor and I, romping, sweating, laughing in my bed that hot Italian summer

84

in Naples. First only the laughter comes back; Eleanor's teeth flashing, Al's broad smile and short, nervous titters as she tickled his small, perfect body. I laughed too, loudest in the tangle of arms and legs and lips and teeth and eyes. How many ways were there to do it? Permutations and combinations, the sheets twisted beneath us drenched with sweat. Eleanor's witch hair stringy and matted with perspiration, the way she used her woman's body like a thing she could dispossess. Flopping, rolling, a wheelbarrow, a dog, a pair of scissors, a fountain spewing, and Al's perfect little body quivering, twitching, becoming more and more excited as Eleanor lost semblance to anything human. She dripped, crawled, padded on all fours, mounting and being mounted, screamed, laughed and flung her witch hair. Eleanor's woman's body, prostrate on the bed throbbing, her hands digging at the pulsing clump of her sex, the witch hair in her eyes, her eyes wider and wider, the purring sound deep in her throat, the pink lips opened and closed dripping. And as I doubled over in a corner of the bed, lost my seed, Al covering her, his perfect little legs thrashing like a swimmer, scrambled into her belly.

Thurley spoke. —Do you remember the night in Naples, the three of us? Al was wary, he knew that night was part of their silence. Thurley continued haltingly. It was my idea, remember, and you were afraid, you warned me, pleaded, even refused. You said I was drunk or crazy, didn't believe Eleanor would do it anyway if you agreed. You didn't believe it till the last minute, did you?

—No, you're right, sometimes I'm not so certain now it happened.

—Then you didn't try to go to her after?

—Of course not, she was your wife. That night was unrepeatable, set off from everything else. It was madness almost, but you, we, decided we could handle it. I wouldn't have dreamed of touching Eleanor unless you knew and approved, and of course I hadn't any reason to believe you would have approved.

—Well, there's something you don't know. I didn't really ever approve. I had no choice.

—Eleanor?

—Yes, benign, sweet, innocent Eleanor. How could you be surprised at anything after her performance?

But it wasn't just hers, I mean all of us together, laughing, enjoying the madness and impossibility. Once I got over the initial shock, I guess you could call it fright, I never doubted the closeness of us all. The marvelous way in which everything became valid, the way touching you or Eleanor was like touching myself, the way just letting go made us all so . . . so . . . I'm fumbling now, I can only recall how it was and try to find the right word, the word that would bring it back, make it happen again for you. I can just stutter really, and point . . .

—Al, Al. Still immaculate. Don't you understand, man, there was nothing spontaneous, nothing new or beautiful, just that woman showing me how helpless I was, showing me how strong she could be, and how I had no way to match her, even prevent her from destroying me.

—Eleanor.

—Yes, yes, yes. Eleanor. I laughed, sure, and after a point I really felt a part of something bigger, a force, a fury, I don't know what exactly, but as soon as it was over, as soon as the three of us were sprawled and empty on the bed, I remembered what I had been laughing and fucking away the whole evening; that it was Eleanor's hate, my wife's hate. She used you, Al, just as she did me. We didn't escape anything that night, we weren't free. She just wanted to show me what she could do to anything I called mine. She killed it, Al. That's why nothing can happen. Why we can't talk. He emptied the glistening tumbler. Al had turned away towards the window.

—But, Bob, why didn't you say something? Afterwards, anytime, before now? It was just a night. We're grown-up people. Nothing changed hands in that silly bed. It was madness, wild, drunken madness. You've let it fester that's all, made it become something it wasn't. Hell, Bob, if she was no good, why would you sacrifice what we had for her? What we had was natural, it was true. You know now for sure Eleanor was sick, real help-needing sick. You did what you could; you held on for as long as any man could without going batty himself. It wasn't your fault, you did all anyone could expect.

—Did I, did I? Maybe I did all I could, but it was what Eleanor expected and needed that counted. I wanted to love her so badly. I wanted anything in her to love. But she was closed, she was methodically, eternally shut away from me. And still she wanted something. I guess she hated me because I tried so hard, because I showed her no matter how hard anyone tried, she could never love or be loved. So she learned to enjoy the slam of the gate down on my fingers when I tried to touch. She would let me get close just to enjoy that sound and my pain, keeping some hope alive, letting me think there was still a chance, then slam. She learned my weaknesses too. The ways I couldn't reach her if I wanted to, and if she would allow me. She used her body, she let me sink in till I could go no further then beg for more, beg, beg, beg, till I bled, then she would begin to rail, say I didn't love her, didn't want her, that I played around, then abuse me, say I wasn't a man, that I was still a big fairy, ask why had I lied, why had I dragged her into a lie of a marriage, abusing, taunting till she laughed, wild, wild, laughter that made me want to die. And if I wouldn't come to her, she'd threaten me, say she'd go out in the street and take the first man she could find. That she'd have his baby, black, brown, red or yellow if she could. Eleanor, that was my Eleanor.

—It's getting late, Bob. Would you rather stay, just sit here a while and talk.

—No. I came to see a show. My story just gets more and more boring. I've been over it so many times it's become incredibly tedious. I wonder how we had patience enough to play out such dull, predictable roles day after day. At the time I even began to pray for some overwhelming catastrophe, some violent explosion, for a demon to enter our lives. Somebody who would stir the pot a bit, somebody who wouldn't be afraid to throw in a handful of blood and guts. So intense when it happened, me wrapped up, full of fear and trembling as if I was involved in some mysterious drama, something resolvable, turning on the most minute perceptions and intuitions. If only I had stepped back, relaxed and read the episodes like I would a bad book. I could have seen how banal, how clinical and poor our lives were. Her moving steadily towards wanton insanity and me creeping back on my hands and knees to little boys. Too pat, just too damned pat.

—Bob . . .

—Nothing to say, Al. Just recalling the days of yore. Do you have a cigarette; I want to coat my lungs, I want to give my mouth something to do besides bleat. I came for a show, not to give one.

—I want to hear you out. Will you come back with me after the service? You know I care about you, Bob. No matter how many times you've said things to yourself, it's not like really getting them off your chest. Give us a chance again. Thurley watched Al's nervous movements as he stood and prepared to go. He seemed wilted. Even behind the indestructible Dacron Al was a weary little dwarf. But Al would take Thurley's burden on his narrow shoulders. Al the de-wifed and de-daughtered would console his matrimonially bankrupt friend. Prince Al the Immaculate returned from the kitchen bearing in his eyes the woe of ages. His regal brow was furrowed, he strode, all melting remorse and sympathy across the field of languishing throw rugs insinuating with a grace beyond the reach of art his perfect arm around Thurley's plump back.

Was it conscience?

TWO

Bette said: —Eddie would you like some more gravy. She slid her spoon into its brown thickness breaking the membrane which like dirty cellophane had formed on its surface. Some more Eddie, she repeated, neither louder nor more insistently simply the words again as she dragged her spoon through the shallow bowl and the thin film disappeared. Bette knew when she began preparing that the tiny Easter ham, two women size, would not make much gravy, nor would it seem a holiday its shrunken redness on the table for Eddie just home. She had be-pineappled its large plate, Libby's slices arranged in rows along the sides, and on its summit brown sugar crust and cloves. Still it had made less than a bowlful of gravy which she spiced and stirred and hoped Eddie would taste. Her brother had been so quiet. When he had returned from the hillside without Brother, it was as if he had been gone another year. Eddie seemed so tired, hardly spoke when he came in the door; just sitting all day till dinner time and then to the table. I was busy in the kitchen, but when I had a minute I'd go in the other room where he sat with Mama. Her in one chair, him in the other. The pup slept beside Mama and I almost believe them too sleeping though their eyes were open, Eddie's always far off out the window and Mama's on Eddie. I'd go in but saying nothing neither me or them it was like a little girl I felt and so silly just standing there in my apron smiling at Eddie till it hurt my face and everything went to pieces and I thought they could feel it and see it too, my face getting sore in front of them because I stood there saying nothing and uglier. I wish

I could have said something. But so strange when I'd go in, felt like I was interrupting them but nothing there but silence, not a word between them. Eddie I should have said how happy we are to have you home, Mama and me are so happy because it's Easter and we have you with us. If I had said it, maybe Mama would be still, maybe she would let me finish, and when she heard, not be able to say different or no. It should be me sometimes who says it. She speaks and because no other voice, what she says is true. I should say things even if she gets mad, even if they are things she doesn't want to hear. I would like to talk about Eugene. Brother can talk about anything. Stories about everybody—about DaddyGene who I barely remember, but when Brother talks sometimes so close, even closer than our real Daddy. Eddie too talked about Eugene and DaddyGene. I wonder why never our father. But I am not sure I could listen; how I can never forget touching him when he had no life. Across miles and miles for days it seemed I moved to touch him that one dead time. I cannot remember another touch, cannot believe he ever lived or held me warm in his arms. It must have been awful to see DaddyGene die. But different because they still talk of him. I am afraid Mama will shout, will tell me not to come in the room again because I stand between them in the way. She makes me know and feel things I wonder if Eddie knows how she makes me feel. It seems he must know with it so strong in that small room, that he would hear her too that way she screams always in my ear to do things and is silent. Bette she is shouting when I stand there Bette get out of this room and leave me with your brother. I felt it so strong he must know. And if he does why doesn't he say no Mama let her stay, why doesn't he say I love her Mama and came to see her too so let her sit with us. I know I must cook. I know I must do things but just let me sit for a moment, let him talk to us both. Mama we need his voice, we need to listen together, to stop the scream that holds us. Let him tell us about Daddy-Gene, about Tiny, about Eugene, and let Brother come too.

92

It will be like Christmas or a birthday party us all laughing and close, and songs Mama and . . . but Mama don't frown. I know you can't dance. I will sit with you while the others dance. I will be more happy than dancing. We can sing while we watch Mama. I do want to be with you more than the wild dance, we will sing Mama and watch. I am not lying.

Eddie heard her the second time she offered the gravy. He poured from the proffered bowl, wetting the mound of potatoes that had hardened on his plate. With his fork he mashed gravy into the yielding lump then poured again into a depression he had patted into its center. Bette watched him perform the familiar operation. Remembered how happy they could be with food. Not just special days, or particular dishes, but the high-chair glee of texture, smell and sound being devoured by the senses. Oatmeal throwing. Eugene finally huge over Eddie a whole bowl on Eddie's big head. Mama then yelling louder than Eddie and both boys up from the table and into the bathroom. Eddie got the hairbrush too and harder too I could tell as it hit splat, splat and soap in his eyes too as Mama washed out the clumps from his hair. It was then we were so close, and Mama always there and sometimes Daddy. Don't cry, Mama, I'll go down and watch, I'll see the mailman first thing and bring it up to you. Don't cry Mama, please don't; they'll be all right.

Eddie raised his spoon. To Bette it seemed to hang for ages, indecisive, wavering as if his arm was caught between tremendous invisible forces which nullified each other in one small pocket of vacuum. She prayed and he swallowed.

It goes down and how many mouthfuls at this table watched in this room. Bette's eyes, Mama's eyes, the eyes of dead Gene, of my father and eyes of the even longer dead some I recall and others even beyond death have watched. Is Mama showing me her day, trying to cover me with the dead emptiness of her life? Is this all there is Mama, this room and this silence? The pup sleeps at her feet. Bette is busy in the kitchen doing the little that keeps them this side of death. Is it to this I have returned? Is Mama trying to show me once and for all what I have to expect? She has shut me in a closet. There is no light, no air. A feeling I thought only came with death, with the heavy lid dropped and the earth in balls beginning to rain. DaddyGene coughed so much I asked him one day if I could help, if I could buy him medicine. He smiled, then laughed loudly with his head thrown back till the coughs began again. I remember the strong smells of him. What I loved to be close to, his thick shirts, the vest stuffed with pipe and tobacco, the hat of soft felt, high crowned always slick and cool inside smelling of leather and darkness when it dropped over my eyes. His smells so different from Mama's softness or my Grandmother Freeda's sweet, powder scent. Then more came.

—Come here you little rascal. The boy could feel the bones in the old man's hand as it wrapped around his shoulder. You afraid of your DaddyGene now boy. The air was stale with the old man's decaying bulk. His feet, too swollen for shoes, were wrapped in layers of ragged wool socks, and when little Eddie approached, their unwashed fragrance made a palpable ring he must enter to touch his grandfather. Gently in a gesture that was full of the knowledge of his own repugnance, the old man drew the boy nearer to his tainted presence. When his grandfather coughed, the boy shuddered, recoiling from both the violence of the rasping explosion and the tightened grip on his thin shoulder as instinctively the huge fingers dug into his flesh. I've been your Papa, you know that don't you boy. I've been as close to one as you've had. Help your mother, boy. You and Gene better help her. Eddie leaned his head against the old man's shoulder. For what seemed hours in the sour cloud, DaddyGene whispered things he couldn't understand into his ears as the boy stood trembling uncontrollably. At last the voice stopped, the hand was removed from his body, and he stood still. Harder and harder to go to his grandfather after that. Even the room came to be avoided. If he calls I will go, but only then. His dripping

94

eyes that are open but sleep. The sound like choking or sobbing when he dozes in the chair. I go to the store for him. From a knotted handkerchief he produces hot, wet coins. I buy him Five Brothers Tobacco which he chews and spits in the basin I must empty. When I carry it I must be very careful. I always wait till the last moment, hoping that this time perhaps it will never fill, and I will not have to carry it to the bathroom. It swishes when I walk; I am afraid it will slosh out on to the floor, as it sways, lap up to touch my fingertips gripping the edges. There is no other way to carry it. A hand on each side, the bowl held out in front of me. I must watch it, for the redness dances in the bowl, and I must not spill it. The toilet is blood color till I flush it away.

He never changes the baggy trousers or the long sleeved undershirt, and he never moves from the chair. His long legs and bloated feet fill the room and the rattle of his breathing.

Even when finally the deep chair empty, I could not enter the room. I could not sleep till tired out from crying over Daddy-Gene's death and finally Mama soft into our room and the pills and the cool glass of water. Down to sleep. Down to sleep. I thought that feeling was only after death, but here Mama sits with the pup sleeping beside her, and I feel it in this room.

Eddie with a clatter that seemed to him malevolently out of proportion and entirely unvolitional replaced his utensil on the side of his plate after raising one forkful of potatoes hashed with gravy to his mouth. Bette's eyes had left him and she tried to busy herself with the tiny portions of ham, potatoes, succotash and coleslaw she had allotted to herself. His mother's plate retained only a grease smear from a tiny slice of ham Bette had served then hastily removed at a look and a gesture from the old woman. Coffee was all she wanted.

—Will you stay now, Edward? His mother's voice was brittle as the fork ringing.

—Yes, Mama, I want to find a job and make a go of it.

—What kind of job? There's only the mill, and they're firing.

—I can go back with the piano man till something else turns up.

—Moving pianos. You know as well as I do what that means. Sitting here, or in some hangout in the Strip till he calls if he ever does. A few dollars a week if you're lucky. Just something to keep you close to that gang of loafers who all call themselves working for the piano man.

—But he does come, Mama, and when he does whatever he pays is something I can contribute to the food money here at home. Besides it's all I can do till some better job turns up.

—Turns up, Edward, and how many jobs have you ever heard of turning up? You threw away the only good job you ever had. Couldn't stay away from those no-goods for eight hours a day. You could still be with the post office and not talking about sitting in some dirty pool room or saloon waiting for the piano man.

—I've told you why I couldn't stay at the post office. You just don't understand, Mama. The same thing day after day after day. I'd get up in the morning, and the first thing I'd see would be those sorting boxes floating in front of my eyes. I knew that if I lived a hundred years each morning they would be sitting waiting for me. More sacks would come into the room as we worked. Never a feeling of getting anywhere or accomplishing anything. Just sack after sack to be emptied and sorted down the proper slot. That would be my life, Mama. It was like a nightmare, like dreaming I couldn't swim and was suddenly dropped in the middle of the sea. I was caught, trapped, didn't have a chance. So much water around me. Sooner or later I knew I had to go under. Fighting just made the nightmare longer. I couldn't take it, Mama. You just don't realize what it meant to face those rows of boxes every morning.

—You're supposed to be a man, Edward. A man works; your grandfather was up every morning and Eugene though he was just a boy. A man does what he can and doesn't make a lot of foolishness for himself by turning things into something they aren't. You talk like a child. What do you want?

Bette whose wad of coleslaw lay forgotten in a corner of her jaw parted her lips as if to speak. But only her eyes furtive under long, lowered lashes participated in the dialogue. She wanted more than anything to say what was at times infinitely close to the precipice of speech.

We had all said the blessing together; Thank the Lord for this food for the nourishment of our bodies sanctified in Jesusname for his sakeamen . . . Me, Eugene, Edward, Mama and Daddy when he was home. But DaddyGene never said it, and sometimes even ate standing up which made Grandmom and Mama so mad. I liked it then, all of us together sitting down three times a day. The blessing was written on the first page of our old Bible. I could say it before I could read and made DaddyGene laugh holding the book while I said it. This Easter Sunday there was nothing to say, just the three of us so long at the table till Eddie had finally lifted his spoon. He seemed to like the gravy, but it's getting cold on his plate. He wants very much to say something, but it's like he's almost dreaming or even like he's left the table to find something, and it's only my brother's shadow I see.

—There must be something more, Mama. When I heard the sacks dropped behind me on the floor, believing in something more was the only way I could go on with what I had to do. I'd tell myself there had to be something more than those dead thuds at my back and the slots waiting.

—It's getting cold, Eddie. The old woman, cut off as she still formed a reply, could only stare incredulously at her daughter's interruption. Involuntarily her brown eyes dropped to her son's plate. It *was* cold there, the white plate showing through as a border between each vegetable even though Bette had served him almost all of the succotash, potatoes and coleslaw. Each item was isolated, even the gravy over the slab of ham had spread sluggishly into a discreet solitary pool. She thought of plates heaped high, of men's laughter, their eyes and jaws devouring like bears. She remembered her heroes at the feast. Now

97

her last son, Eddie, was poised over the meagre Easter supper. Cold. Cold. His shadow across the dish, him leaning towards her, a little boy again and almost he understands, almost he seems to be ready to speak. *Her* sad eyes, the delicate forehead you could see the bones so clean beneath. Come, come, son, she wanted to say if only he would . . .

—There must be more, Mama, there must be.

And he died there, halfway. Her lover would never return. Only shoes, only a worn razor strap still hanging on a bathroom nail, only his straight razor still shining on the bureau and the dark mug and brush. Asks too much, he asks too much. Can I fill another table, this flesh dry and bones strengthless, legs tied to cold metal. Can I rise, does he think I can wait for him. There is no breast to pillow his head, no soft lap where he may bow or sit. Can I even stand without the steel clutched tight in my hand. And is there anything to give even if I would give, even if I could forget, is there even time to wait again?

—Cold, Eddie, it's getting cold.

Something roared in the old woman's ears. It rose a crescendo of surging, deep throated sound. Like sea shells clamped to both ears the room possessed her in its blank ubiquitous rhythm. From some unknown source, far out of her own experience and reaching back to a dark communal fund of impulse she sensed the warning of this ocean sound. The deadness below her waist climbed inch by inch to turn her whole body into stone. It was only Bette's hands on her shoulders and the violent rocking of her body back and forth in her son's grasp that woke her to the sound of her own low keening—Nothing . . . nothing . . . nothing . . . nothing . . .

Eddie walked slowly down Dumferline Street. His head was bowed and he watched his feet, playing the old game of snake-in-the-crack, avoiding seams and splits in the broken pavement. Streets weren't fixed very often in his neighborhood so his progress was giddy and irregular as he side-stepped and strode like a wino, like he had seen his father coming home or in anger head for the Strip.

He remembered the other street. When he was younger and his father worked regularly, and they had moved for a short while into the little island of Negro families within the white sea of respectability. Eddie recalled his friend, Joel, who timidly from the others had slipped away to join the dark newcomer.

Half that street was lined by tall, prosperous trees, oaks and wide chestnuts oddly out of place because the sidewalks had begun to crack and large houses deteriorate. Half was brick, the other wood. When only white people had lived on the street, the passage from one end to another had been difficult, but it was a pleasant division reminding some how far they'd come and promising others a rich reward if they just kept at it. Regularly the wooden end was abandoned. No one came there to stay; it was rather a watering place, a station for the transient white families moving up along invisible threads of prosperity. *For sale,* then *For rent* signs blossomed predictably as the chestnuts at the other end. Almost everyone managed to move, if not to the brick and stone of Carter Street, then some other shaded street, road or avenue. But one day the stores and shops began to get too close. Too many strange cars were parked beneath the chestnuts, or blocking driveways. Privacy disappeared and Negroes moved into the wooden end. Everyone else who could moved out, leaving behind a few old people who were too tired to run, a sick, lonely widower who was too proud, and in the corner apartment building the permanent outsiders who hadn't noticed or didn't care.

Beneath the wide chestnut trees, Joel and Eddie had walked. Old Mr. Duncan had chased them one day with a broom. He had called Joel a sneakin' pink nigger, trembling and stuttering as he protected his buckeyes. The widower's porch had been painted again, a bright, tulip yellow this time. Not a brick was out of place or crumbling in his side of a terra-cotta duplex. His lawn was even greener than usual after the rain, its neat border of pastel flowers calm and formidable as a moat. He never spoke to anyone who passed his porch, yet his eyes missed nothing, and from his green and white wicker chair he silently judged. The Corries who lived next door to him were probably at Foxes Tavern getting drunk. If they got very drunk, they would return home and fight, usually icing their evening with a naked wrestling match, all the lights on and blinds up which Eddie and Joel had watched many evenings.

The wide chestnuts were a canopy, then the boys were beneath an oak with its peeling bark. Eddie usually ran up the alley when he wanted to meet Joel at the white end of the street. He would yell up from the apartment building's small back court where the garbage cans stood, hoping he would not run into old Mr. Pope, the janitor, whom Joel called Pops and who always looked at Eddie so strangely. One day Mr. Pope had ordered him to stay out of the court. Eddie had been afraid, but later realized the short, black man couldn't really order him to do anything. Next time he saw Mr. Pope he too called him Pops. The old man had turned away, muttering something under his breath, but after that never another word. Many times as he had been standing in the court waiting for Joel to come down, the Negro boy knew old man Pope's eyes were watching him. He would feel skittish, almost on the verge of running, not afraid of anything the old man would do, but ashamed of what he had done to Mr. Pope. Also those secrets he knew and used on Mr. Pope were secrets about himself and here, where the old man talked and lived with white people everyday, the secrets were in danger.

It was strange, how the trees made noise, yet nothing could be seen moving them. Walking beside Joel, trying to hide and forget till he was past the brick houses, Eddie wondered why he feared an old man and not these very trees under which he moved. Surely the old black man knew no more, nor could speak to the white people more plainly than these trees. In fact, who would listen to him; Mr. Pope too was of another kind, an im-

100

penetrable growing thing that neither dreamed, loved, nor re-membered. These trees if someone knew how to listen would reveal as much. How Eddie had battered them with sticks to get buckeyes, shuffled through their leaves, carved his name and initials after dark into their thick trunks. Had they seen him crouched at night in the alley, had they seen what he did to him-self as he watched the Corries. The trees were tall and surely knew.

One evening snow had fallen. A soft white layer over every-thing, creating fantastic shapes, making his walk home with a quart of milk under his arm something new. Everything had seemed smaller, a shrunken world, and intimate, a mystery shared that had made him closer to the loaded trees and padded sidewalks. As if everyone was black one morning, or white or any color that covered and completed the past. Church music, like bells at first but then his own church people singing. He had smiled feeling the soft snow blot against his skin. All away, all washed away, closer, nearer. Had the trees seen him then, that night they had dipped so low, and he had walked through a gleaming tunnel? Did they remember green now, and damply beginning to stir how close he had been to joy, how near to weeping? What could he tell the others when he had finally gone home? Yes, I've been a long time in the cold, yes, I have a chill, and you waiting all the time for this milk. But don't sit down, don't open and drink it, go out, no come out with me, there's something you should all see. Just come with me, you don't even need coats, just walk up the street, beneath those big trees full of snow, it's not like it usually is, not like the valley, or the shadow of death, no Mama, no Gene and Bette, it's . . . it's . . . But you set down what you went for and go stand by the gas stove.

His mother's sobs re-echoed in his ears. It was the sound of all despair, totally unanswerable, a sound whose sapless roots drained the substance of hope. Would Alice be home, would she want to see him? He had asked Brother not to tell. Again the

101

same secrecy with her as with his mother and sister. Vaguely he sensed a common motive, something behind this trip home with which he conspired. In a way it was another Eddie, a shadow Eddie who had learned to live unseen. They had talks together, these two Eddies, and from the shadow much had been learned. Grierson had been right, the cure had restored some lost part, but could the shadow be lived with, did the shadow want to live?

Snap! Just missed the poison of that one. Slowly but surely it gets to be my time. Night comes. The air is different isn't it? I mean for you it probably doesn't matter much, but I have bad memories of heavy day air and sunshine that chokes. You see I was sick when I was younger. Always weaker and teased. Too soft because I let their nonsense eat me up. My brother was the worst, I guess because he was my brother and different because he was bigger, stronger and was loved. Not that she didn't love me. No, don't pay any attention to what just happened back there. She was upset. And at her age and in her condition (she was always strong before, tough and not afraid even when twins came too soon after Eugene and died, two more kids without a whimper of fear) it's so hard to do anything about what she feels strongly. I can understand that. Sometimes I feel like I'm in a glove, or a bag like Brother says. You must love Brother, no matter what else, you must love that ugly bastard. No, when she screams and says those terrible things about Bette and about me, it's just something boiling over that has to come. Better in fact that it does. It's her nerves, her feelings using her, like they've been used. She holds things in, so when they come, they have to be violent, tear their way out. I don't mind really. I thought it might be like this. It's Bette more than myself I feel sorry for. She's never had a chance. I helped make Mama what she is. I was soft and easy too long, she held me like she holds Bette now. She needed someone, I mean after Daddy and Eugene had gone she needed someone. So I stayed on and on, doing what I could. But she just got worse, and I began to understand no matter how hard I tried, I couldn't be Eugene, and

102

when she was worst that's all she wanted, that's all that could help her. My dead brother. So I inched away, little by little. Bette was getting old enough to do what had to be done, and better too since she was a girl, and since nobody could do or be what Mama really wanted, I got away. But I did harm, I tried to keep it from her but somehow she found out. She always blamed the others, especially Brother; she didn't understand it was something that had to happen. A man just can't live day after day on nothing. And drinking, after a while you get sick before you get high drinking bad stuff and the belly ache and head throbbing when you wake up afterwards drives you nearly mad and you can't get any help because the thought of the stuff that's made you the way you are is sickening so you just suffer and the world won't turn off. One thing leads to another; what's it matter whose idea, or who gives you the first one, and before you know it hooked. And so what, there's nothing so big it can't be shut out, and after a while the world is only a dream. But sometimes I thought of Mama, and the dream got to be a bad, bad dream. It hurt my guts like drying-out days once did. One morning wind up in a cell, nothing to be had, they look at you like an animal and come to watch when it gets so bad you start climbing the wall. You beat your head on the stones, on the floor of that cage, you try to twist your neck off between the bars. But nothing breaks, nothing gives. Just them like in a zoo so you can't quite kill yourself. I remember how finally sleeping the dreams I had. And someone screaming Mama, Mama in my ear so loud I thought my head would split, and then it was just me in that cage, my own mouth going, calling her. You shiver and sweat and you try to sit still, but pieces of your body flop out and scrape themselves along a razor. You watch them squirming, bleeding and you know it's you and you feel it, and nothing so bad as when they return and crawl back in your guts, full of pieces of glass, splinters and stones.

So she had to know. And it hurt her. She wouldn't say anything. Just be sitting when I came in looking so old in that shawl and legs like sticks in braces. It was her eyes following me.

Why do we have to fight? Don't we understand all we have is each other? I can't believe is the same place, not the same place as before. DaddyGene was so big in the chair, Eugene and I playing, Bette in the playpen sucking her thumb. It was different air, different colors then, as big as the world, but so easy to move in, to find things, to laugh or be quiet and alone. My little sister, Bette, all lumps and flaps yelling from her playpen, the rows of colored beads alive in her pudgy hands as she squealed and bounced so fast then plopping down on her lumpy seat and up again sometimes crying, sometimes laughing. We could make her cry or laugh, Eugene and I when nobody watched could play her like a game. We knew which strings to pull, which toy to steal, where it tickled and where she didn't like our hands. It was funny how easy she forgot. How she would always smile when we came to her, though we were ashamed and felt we wouldn't be forgiven. On our knees making faces through the bars she'd pat our cheeks, pinch our noses, kiss us till we made funny noises then stamp her foot and jump like a little monkey in her flannel all-covering pajamas with a lump and big buttons in the back. Mama calls her hussy and a whore. She said Brother snuck round the house, and she could hear them at night like prowling cats from her bed when they thought she was asleep. And said Bette had always been that way, that after her father and DaddyGene had gone there was no keeping boys from her fast womanish ways. Coming at night like cats—Bette cried still, she cried not because it was true, but because it was Mama who said such things, and there was no answer because Mama's words would never change. She was there, still there as always and never, never could she be denied.

Things she said about me. Not like about Bette, not warped, crazy things but like my own voice accusing. So why do we have to fight? Did I come back for this, did I go away, did I die for that year just for this? I couldn't expect her to believe quickly. Not after everything she's seen, surely she has a right to doubt, to wait before she opens her arms again. She is an old woman, so much of her life is dead. For her, when they said I was in jail, that I had sunk as low as she knew I had all along, I died. What we had before hadn't been much, no, to move even slightly from her was to destroy almost everything, but after the news, after the disgrace I put to the name of her dead, there was nothing. Can I hope someday she will forgive?

Eddie side-stepped avoiding a pit of nodding snakes. Their throats were swollen, forked black worms darted from bullet heads. How many nights down this street? How many trips along this broken path before a man was old? Stick ball here, a football spiralling perfect as a bird, then dying as it touched his fingertips, his crane legs for once taking the prize. He hoped so badly Alice would be home, that like Brother she would be waiting unchanged, even in the same clothes, as if time were never more than the space between a glance away and back.

He could tell Alice. She would understand how it hurt him to fight, how senseless everything was that kept Mama deep in her own pain.

Alice, do you love? As close as we come to understanding. Lights coming on around me. Same switches, but different hands. Beneath and above like at home, the dirt swatches from countless hands moving in darkness, going too far, falling short. And children who can't quite reach but try. Alice turning out the light. Mama turning out the light. The orderly in white turning out the light. The bartender on turning the light. To sleep they all meant. No more love, no more frowns, no more needles, no more booze, to sleep, to sleep. Alice beside me I never dream. It must be my hand on her buttock as I sleep. I stir never either. Hand on her buttock, sleeping on my belly like when a kid I think because she does too on her belly like little Bette arms and legs sprawled like a frog the big buttoned lump sitting high my hand on it. Strange how deep it seems sometimes. Split deepness if I lift the covers and peek. My hand on the soft mound deep sleeping like a baby. Funny how one fingertip touch can feel everything. The slope of flesh hill, its softness, its deep cleft, even where it goes to fuzz and its soft color one fingertip resting can know. Please be Alice.

Around him lights came on. It was night Eddie liked, his time. He stepped gingerly avoiding cracks, Eddie snake dancer bold and unafraid. Jungle birds shrieked around him, their brazen calls summoning night spirits. Sweet breathed panthers slunk invisible on padded feet, only eyes through the thick undergrowth. Something huge and steel taloned had made a kill and bellowed the blood call to its mate. Monkeys on lace branches gibbered nervously at the moon. Eddie leapt the coiled bulk of a python.

Other nights. The wild chase night and Mama like always waiting. What had happened, when did it begin? Certain things returned clearly. He felt his hand glide into the past, experienced the cold, metallic sensation of that long ago night's coins in his hand:

Eddie had removed his last fifty cents from his drawer. Two dimes, a nickel and a quarter. At the field they'd probably be playing blackjack. He could get in for at least five hands, and he had never lost five straight before. Joel would be there too, not playing as usual, but sitting at the top of the stairwell watching for cops. That was worth a quarter win or lose, and Joel seemed content with cutting the first five pots for his due. Eddie told his mother he didn't feel well and wanted to skip supper, but she was unsatisfied.

—You can't even sit down long enough to eat your supper. You sure do love that bunch of roughnecks, don't you? I don't want you staying away from here late either. I know what you all do down at that field. Don't think I don't know. And don't expect nothing to be here for you to eat when you get home, if you can't sit down with the rest of us, just take your chances.

—I told you I didn't feel good. I won't be wanting nothing.

—But you feel good enough to go runnin' off to that bunch of white hoodlums. Your father and I work hard to keep you in a decent neighborhood, and how do you show your appreciation, by running with the lowest pack of rats you can find. I have a mind to make you stay right here.

Eddie listened and hoped she would begin again and stop soon at a better point to walk out on. After a while, no matter how right he knew he was and how unreasonable all her arguments, his resolution would weaken. It was simply her. His mother loving him in the only way she could that he could not deny. So much had been lost in that short space of silence between them. Strange how first his body, then his mind had become ashamed before her. It was almost as if the words he had learned had made things different. The word for his sex, the word for his tears, his love, his fear. No, nothing had changed, but a subtle alienation made communicating any small piece of himself as difficult as it had once been easy to give the whole. If he could somehow begin, master the first word which would soften her eyes, make her understand how much he still needed and loved. But instead he waited for a cue, a sign she had exhausted herself and would give up again trying to penetrate by violence the thin shell between them.

—Mom, I won't be late. I promise. And I got a quarter if I get hungry later. She was gone before the quarter was produced. He felt it would have been better somehow if she had waited to see it. But now whatever she wanted to believe could remain undisturbed.

Evening hadn't cooled the city. He had watched a long time before venturing his fifty cents. The stakes were only a dime, but he dropped a quarter down on board for show. The streetlights came on, and in two hours he had a pile of silver in front of him and had won the deal. He had been lookout before he entered the game, but now Joel had arrived and took up his regular seat. Eddie's streak continued, paying off only twice in ten rounds and matching the only blackjack he dealt with one of his own. The other players were growing steadily broke and disgusted. Cordigan, one of the older boys, whose blackjack had lost, visibly squirmed each time the dealer turned over his card. Cordigan had big hands with short fingers, and hair had already begun to cover their backs. He watched the Negro boy gather up the cards, raking in a dime from each player who had failed to beat his nineteen.

—Hey boys, don't you think it's about time we had us a new dealer? Cordigan's thick hands were spread out on his knees, a square signet ring, gold and ruby eyed, reflected the streetlamp. His tone contained no question. Beside him the thinner figure of Ken leaned further into the light. His crew cut and windbreaker matched Cordigan's, but no one except Ken ever noticed they were the same.

—I think you're right, Cordy. Yeah, I think maybe you should deal a while. I mean just till things even up a bit.

—What are you guys talking about? That ain't no guarantee of nothing. I got a little hot streak, that's all. Somebody's bound to get blackjack soon.

—Well, I already got blackjack once, and you had the deal long enough.

—It's only fair it should go to the one who had blackjack last.

—But I ain't lost it yet. The cards were in a neat stack in front of Eddie. He looked around at the five deeply shaded faces like masks in the dark stairwell. One cigarette was burning. He couldn't tell how the others had reacted to Cordigan's demand. What his flunky Ken said didn't really matter if the others were not on Cordigan's side. Eddie began to slowly shuffle the deck.

—Never mind that, I mix up my own deal. Cordigan's hand reached towards him.

The Negro continued to shuffle, slowly at the level of his stomach his hands filtered through the deck, his eyes fixed on the ruby eye suspended in the darkness. All other movement

108

had stopped; the glowing cigarette had disappeared; each player sat rigid as the stone stairs on which they were ranged.

—Gimme the cards, kid, you've had it. Cordigan's lips were blue, then his mouth was a black hole in his face. Eddie knew Cordigan could take what he wanted from him, and there was really no question about submitting, but for once in the glittering coins he had won a piece of the white boy he wouldn't give up.

—Sure, take 'em Cordy. I gotta go anyway, I promised my mother I'd be home.

—Did you hear that? Sambo's won everybody's money and now all the sudden he gotta git home to his Mammie. Well, you can go if you want to, but leave the dough. The tableau had come to life. Each stone figure had imperceptibly closed in on the Negro. Ken, Harry, Ronnie, Skeets and Cordigan were all one now, aroused by a magic word that had been spoken. The cards stopped moving, it was suddenly cold, and Eddie feared that soon the streetlight would blaze one bright time then be snuffed out. He was shivering and his hands wanted something solid to grasp. He could feel the circle tightening, it was a belt around his waist, around his head that began to cut the flesh.

It ain't right you guys. Cordigan ain't got no right, Skeets, Harry, you know I'd stick by you. And he knew that he wouldn't if it had been one of them, and he knew they wouldn't because Cordigan . . .

—Cards, Sambo . . .

It was cold in the stairwell, in the arc of the streetlamp, and she knew what went on down there and Joel sitting quiet above. Of the players, Eddie was closest to the top and could make it if he ran quickly. Sambo. Sambo. Sambo. Run Tiger.

He scooped up as much as he could in one hand, straightening and pitching the cards into Cordigan's blue face. Then it was him running, running in a leap over the hedges, handful of money, their heavy footfalls behind, curses and loud breath be-

109

hind that would never catch him as he stretched headlong into the wind freer than he had ever been, down the street and into the alley with the wind, handful of money singing because they never would catch him. He would easily outdistance them, and this night, heart thumping, he had won the pile and would keep it silver beside him as he slept. It was bright now, moon bright and under his feet the ground crunched and was gone. Cool, clear, he could even smell the wind and hear his heart, till up the steps in two bounds the screen door would slam behind him and he would sleep heart-still until tomorrow when they would find him, beat him, and take it all back.

She was waiting when the door flung open. Almost immediately her words flew in his face. —Where have you been, boy?

—Nowhere Ma, I mean just at Joel's house, just there talking with Joel.

—Talking about what, and what are you shaking all over for? Are you running with those hoodlums again? Look at the time boy. I been sitting here waiting for you since ten o'clock. Why won't you behave? Off with them wild white boys again. Don't you know by now they's just gonna hurt you? Don't you know by now? Since ten o'clock worrying my heart out. Why won't you act right?

—I told you I was just with Joel, Mama.

—With Joel doing what till near one o'clock in the morning.

—I don't know, I mean we was just sitting, talking. I didn't notice at all how late it was.

—Well next time just stay out all night with your white friend. If he can come and go as he pleases, it don't mean you can. Just cause he can run his mother to death, ain't no reason for you both to start on me. Next time you stay out like this, don't come home expecting somebody to be waiting on you. She knew she had to wait, and she knew she would wait again, tomorrow, or the next day, she would always be there.

—Listen to me, boy. Her eyes no longer flashed. As she spoke the animation left her gestures, her features and her voice. The calm and tears that followed were just as predictable as the outburst had been. He watched the one subside and the other gradually take possession of her body. Martha sat down again, sinking into the battered armchair facing the hallway where Eddie still stood. She had nothing else to say, those three hours dozing, snapping awake, pulling the gray cotton sweater closer around her shoulders. She had been a very old woman all that time, she had been very old and grew older, grayer as each minute passed. She railed at him because he had heaped these years on, and now she would cry because only in his young, strong body or in Eugene's could they be borne away. Why was it so hard? Why must she always sit and wait? Staring at doorways, down streets, straining her ears for a footfall, her eyes for a headlight or a figure through the haze. Sometimes she thought she could feel the lines etching their way into her face, she felt things being taken away, felt herself losing the few subdued female beauties of her body that were all of the past she retained, although into that past she had poured everything. She knew for her sons, for the men they would soon be, she could never be a woman. Never create that mysterious, transforming presence for them. She had never been beautiful, never more than attractive and that only to some men, but it wasn't this attraction that her sons denied. Clarence would still come back to her, moved by desire, and it was still something she could believe was uniquely her own that aroused him. At least it was what they made themselves believe, and accepting it as such made it true. What her sons denied was not that she had been a woman, or was one now, but that she would remain one. Her posture in the chair, sweater pulled tightly across her shoulders had been forced on her by them. What she had realized in that chair, and too many times before, was that she was losing the essential, necessary sense of anticipation. Waiting for someone, for something had always been bearable because faith had supported her worst sufferings. In her bed of pain, each time it had been a child she waited for, even when the twins had come too early dying within three days of each other, there had been faith in a next time, in that strong baby, Eugene, already at home. Her faith had been justified, others came, strong, healthy to grow up beside her. Now with her youngest son a different kind of faith was required. There was nothing to anticipate, he had been suckled, clothed, she had given dutifully and unselfishly to his life and now . . . now he would leave, leave her behind just as readily as birds do the dried, broken straw they've outgrown. And what did she have to look forward to? There had been no great illumination, no bliss or unconfined rapture at any point in the long struggle with her sons. They had been conceived, born, and both would soon be gone, leaving only pain. She had believed that someday she would receive her due. Not selfishly something given her in return for suffering, but simply the answer to why she had suffered. The climaxes, the up and down moments of joy and sorrow were afterall too little to believe in. Something told her all these momentary feelings must lead to a complete and final resolution which she by suffering could deserve to understand. But each time she waited, what came, if anything at all did, was never enough. No flash of light, no deep, settled contentment or despair, only the tickled nerve end dance leading her on and on, an animal pursuing the carrot on the end of a stick. There had been love, then God, then love again, and now God up once more on the seesaw holding out this man-child, beckoning her to continue again, to wait. But she was growing too tired, she would sit down one day without waiting just because she was so tired. She would find her sweater, go to her chair and forget time.

She wept now because she had risen to the bait again. She had strained her body and mind, grabbed at the boy as if he was the last thing above water into which she was sinking. But perhaps he would carry her through, perhaps God too was waiting, trying her to the end of her strength the way he tried all his saints. Perhaps too, some miracle would carry her to another shore, a far off golden beach where the sun shone, and fruit hung heavy with ripeness on golden branches. Perhaps someday she would be vomited up suddenly in paradise.

—You know your father's going to be up soon, if he sees you haven't been to bed yet, you know there'll be trouble. She felt foolish now, foolish for doubting, for ever believing that great day wouldn't come. He was still a little boy; he stood the way he always had, like Eugene, waiting for a word or a motion from his Mama to climb up and settle himself in her lap, to be forgiven or reassured, to be freed or received.

—I was just talking with Joel, Mama. I'm sorry . . . I forgot the time . . . talking cause he couldn't sleep.

—Like I did with you when you had bad dreams.

—Yes, like that, only . . . She saw him remembering, realizing what she had said. He stopped speaking, and his eyes avoided hers. She anticipated a word, knowing at the same time what it would be, what it would begin. He took a step towards her, she saw his lips purse, and slowly reappear full and moistened. The word had to come.

Eddie's gaze dropped; the coins were greasy in his tight fist. He quickly turned and mounted the steps as quietly as he could, but Martha heard each stair receive the weight of his body, even thought she heard his breath as he moved cautiously through the darkness. Her husband would be up soon for work, she would wait for him here, in the chair.

Alice the dancer. She had taken reluctant Eddie to the ballet school. All white but them. Never so close to one before, the white girls' arms with light down that covered the flesh when close enough to see. The thought of one in his arms. How his knees had shaken. But Alice really the best dancer. So easy, so free, really the queen as she had soared or pirouetted or stretched her body to the half ugly, half impossible contortions that had names, but Eddie didn't know. Every week on Saturdays they had gone. Hadn't seen Alice much after she had won the scholarship and gone off to school. A rare bird. So ugly Alice was you knew she was Brother's sister, but when she returned something different, something standoffish that made you want to go to her. Alice had come back more beautiful than Eddie had seen anyone. And she had taken him to watch her ballet lessons. The first few times they had talked, nothing much, all they could say were old things, stuff about when they were kids, and what they had said seemed really about Eddie but an Alice who had died and had nothing to do with either person sitting on the glider. Eddie was always with Brother so he had seen Alice often. It was on the porch of the Smalls' frame house where Alice lived and Brother sometimes slept that they would meet. One day she had just popped up and asked so he went with her to the school, met her friends and broadcast his awkwardness.

On benches in the red backed booth of a soda fountain. Eddie, Alice, group of her fellow dancers, coffee, Cokes ranged on a checkered oilskin cloth. His eyes in his cup Eddie had listened. Talk, talk, talk, how they could talk. Everything, anything. Shameless even. What Eddie kept to himself, what he would rather watch swimming in his plastic cup, private and limp like the light bulb reflected on the black coffee's surface. He had stirred his plastic spoon round and round listening. Clara had talked:

—Why it's getting better every day. My youngest sister told me that a Negro had been elected president of her high school class. That's people for you. A few years ago when I was in ponytail and saddle shoes, there weren't any colored students there at all. I bet half my contemporaries believed colored boys had tails. A nervous semblance of laughter passed from face to face. It stopped on both sides of Eddie who never heard or saw it, black coffee staring. Just give people a chance. We have so much in common, and I mean essentials; the emotions, the spirit, the potential for suffering and transcendence, things embedded too deeply to be erased by superficial distinctions of race or religion. I sincerely believe this; everything points to its truth.

Just look around. Take this group—if I say *pain,* everybody here knows what I mean. Maybe it doesn't connote precisely the same words to each of us, but we do share the fundamental reality of this concept, grasp it intuitively as part of the human experience. It's this sort of perception, this community of souls, if you please, that in the end will obliterate intolerance. Clara had shown her bad teeth. Her eyes had surveyed the audience, resting just an iota longer on Alice and Eddie with the undergraduate rhetorician's instinct for emphatic pause. The silence had brought Eddie's head up long enough for him to hear, *Just men and women in the world,* before he had returned to plumb the depths of his cold coffee, futilely fishing for the pinpoint of light with his plastic spoon.

Alice had asked him later why he hadn't listened or joined in the discussion. He could tell she was displeased, even embarrassed. He had felt the good thing between them loosen, the cold, bright aloofness of an unfamiliar Alice returning. They had swayed together on their glider, barely moving, Alice avoiding his face, her hands in her lap. The glider had squeaked, and Eddie felt it all slipping away, had wanted to grab little Alice, pull her hair or take her toy or throw dirt or push her down in the grass. Where was little Alice, old Alice who word by word, evening by evening on the loud glider had been coming back? His new, beautiful Alice. Going, going . . .

—I thought I recognized something different in you, Edward. Something I could respond to. I don't quite know what. Going away has made some things very difficult for me. I suppose I expected too much. But this afternoon, I don't know what I wanted, this afternoon I wanted everyone to . . . to . . . appreciate you. I didn't want to put you on display, but I wanted to reassure myself, I think that's what it was, reassure myself. I wanted to be certain I wasn't fooling myself, that I wasn't just lonely and weak making you something you weren't and didn't want to be. Do you understand me, Edward? It's been hard since I've come back. And in many ways I believe you know exactly how I feel. At least I hope you know, and that's why it's been good to be with you. Why I see you and no one else in the neighborhood. It's not that I think I'm better, it's just that I have absolutely nothing to say to them. I feel like a fish out of water. But I know this is my water, my home, that I can't ever change. And I want so much to have someone to share what I've learned, to have it flourish here. A person to help me keep alive the little something different I've felt grow up in me. Someone to preserve it, to protect it. I don't want to fall back, back into this . . . Her arms had stretched out, wide, wide, wide. She had leaned forward stopping the glider's motion, her arms straining, her fingertips stiff in the effort of expansion. As if the *this* could be embraced, as if she could wrap the *this* in her stretched arms and smother it. She stood, abruptly rising on her toes, her slim dancer's body a cross. As if overburdened by a sudden, immense weight her arms had dropped stiffly to her sides. Eddie had caught her, afraid she was going to fall. He had never been held so tightly.

They had fucked that night in dead Mr. and Mrs. Small's big bed. During the night they had heard Brother come in and immediately begin to snore as he passed out on the sofa. The dancing lessons had continued. Eddie watched and listened . . .

Please be there. Please forgive. Through the shabby streets Eddie the beggar moved. His motion the torpitude of a snail. Behind, his gleaming spore undulated, slowly being devoured by snakes. His margin of safety was diminishing, the sharp tongues would momentarily be at his hind parts. His eleemosynary chalice rattled in his hand. He believed it would frighten away the night crawlers. There was one coin left.

He knocked.

He knocked again . . .

He knocked again . . . and Alice answered. As if from a ghost she shied back. Alice ugly in the half-light. Her flowing robe was something of her long dead mother's. Eddie remembered Mrs. Small vaguely. Mrs. Small who bore white Brother and brown Alice no one would believe from the same man.

Is it my Alice? May I begin to speak? No one will ever know how difficult on this doorstep it is to begin.

—Hello, Alice.

—Hello, Eddie.

—I've come back.

—I knew you would, but I didn't expect you this evening. It was oddly dark behind her. A simple house, a box, wall, corridor. Brother's couch still there, a bulk beneath the window broken-backed. Tiny lamp burning on an end table, only source of light except for the thin stripe along the bottom edge of the bedroom door. Should he try to kiss her? How long had it been?

She switched on more light. Around her pulling tighter the aged chenille robe. Something old, something pink left by a dead woman. Did Eddie really know that?

—It's been a long time. Had you forgotten?

—No, Eddie, not forgotten you or how long either. Please sit down, I was reading, I'll turn out the light. The gown showed her trim ankles, and as she reached into the bedroom feeling for a switch it revealed the beginning swell of her dancer's calf. How long have you been home? I hadn't heard you were back. Does William know? Eddie hated to hear her call Brother *William*; it was like telling a lie. Brother was Brother, he was alive. William was a ghost dwelling only in Alice's mind and here in the house of the dead Smalls. He was suddenly irritated, so vexed that for a moment he forgot the calf.

—Did they cut out your tongue down there or are you just ignoring me? Eddie still stood. Beneath the frayed pink chenille he could see the free mounds of her breast.

—I just got in today. Mama was so excited, things just wouldn't go right. I thought I'd better leave early and let her get her rest, and I thought I'd come to see you. It's you I've wanted to see for so long anyway. Just for a minute, if you're not busy.

—Why come here? For what, Eddie? You didn't come to say good-bye before you left so why bother to come now? Emphasizing the last word, she sunk wearily into the swayback couch. Her eyes were tired, tired Alice eyes, brown staring at sudden Eddie standing awkward in her livingroom.

—Didn't you, didn't you get my note? I gave it to Brother, and he promised he'd bring it to you . . .

—That, oh yes. I received it. William with all the solemnity proper to the occasion delivered it with bated breath and downcast countenance. She smiled, a strange un-Alice smile at Eddie. He shivered and wished for the half-light again.

—I came back because I love you, Alice.

—Like you loved Clara?

—Please, Alice, what's done is done. I made a mistake, I've made lots of mistakes, but it's now I have to live for. Now, when all you have to say is I forgive to begin again. All the time when I was away and just now at home when Mama sat there staring at me, it was you that kept me from screaming, the thought of you that . . .

—You're running from your mother aren't you, Eddie? She drove you away didn't she? Just like Clara, your Mama's finished with her Eddie boy so you come to good Alice. Well, you've come to the wrong place. I'm expecting company.

—Company?

—Yes, Eddie, company, a gentleman caller if you wish. I said I remembered, but you took for granted what I remembered. See if Clara's home, Eddie. See if she welcomes you with open arms, and Mr. Rawlins, and Clara's mother. You'd better try the back door first, don't shock them too much all at once.

—You can't forget can you? One night, Alice, one lousy night. Clara getting her kicks and me like a fool obliging. I didn't think you'd ever know, and even if you did, I didn't see how you could care. She's a tramp, you know that. She just wanted a toss in the hay.

—With her black buck. With you so she could smile and proclaim it. So she could prove her principles with what she has between her legs. No, no I didn't care, it didn't matter to me sitting listening every time she opened her mouth to how real it was, to how meaningful it was, to all the essential truths it demonstrated about men and women. Her glib, bitch mouth so full of praise for Edward, how tender he was, how understanding, how it didn't make any difference in the world what color he was. No . . . It didn't matter; I didn't care.

—Once, Alice, once, I swear it. That's all. I never touched her again.

—Do you think it matters—how many times mattered. I gave you something, I trusted you, Eddie. And all I gave you were willing to trade with that whore for a smell of her white ass. Something rose in Alice and burst. She cried, bitterly and for an age it seemed before Edward moved to her side on the sinking couch. Little Alice sobbed in his arms, cuddling closer, not to him, but to the soft, yielding presence on which her sorrow leaned. Her lost Eddie, home again, home again who whispered.

—I love you, Alice . . . I love you, Alice, please don't cry, please Alice, don't cry. The robe fell away. Her hand which had held it together circled Eddie's neck. It had been long, futile anger. It's closeness choked her, and she knew Eddie far away was pained by its distant force. Intenerating grief. How she buried him beneath the maleflesh she pulled round her like a hood. Eddie gone, dying his way. That night Brother dragged him back, and she knew they had been taking it, and Eddie moaned all night like a child having nightmares; she had watched him tossing in a stupor, his body beside her brother's in the dark room. Oh, for the strength to lift him, to carry him clean and refleshed into her bed. Poor trembling Eddie, the white flesh still reeking from his contaminated body. Oh, to have the arms to raise him, my Eddie, once more from the floor, from the dark room. But how after her can I touch, how can I give again what he had destroyed. Week after week, she

119

saw in William's eyes the cold, unforgiving blame. Eddie had promised, he had tried, kept the piddling job moving pianos; he had been so decent, but after she had refused him, the poison ran through his veins again. Then really gone, not just held off by her anger, the searing anger, the anger supportable only because she believed she had the power to relent, but by the remorse he left solid inside her, like a burning coal when he left, and it was too late for her to forgive. A year could be so long. And after a while the nights are interminable. Worst then when emptiness must be close. When emptiness is a cold, palpable thing you can touch on the sheet beside you. How long? Till like a parade they came. Her lovers. The gates were open, emptiness was a face, a body beside her, long, tall, short, fat, and did it matter afterall that emptiness had a name. She had enough. But they always came back. Like a parade, in shining uniforms, neat, clean, always punctual and well groomed, her men, her lovers, her emptiness.

The robe parted to her waist. Her breasts were powder dusted, in the cleft a few tiny hairs grew. Eddie lowered his head, felt the dark nipple brush his cheek, the faint bumping of her heart. How long had it been?

He eased her down, slowly, slowly, the robe off her shoulders, a faded pink cloud beneath her naked body. He dipped and kissed, his pursed lips tracing the length of her body, the hot house smells kaleidoscoping, filling his nostrils in a hundred shades from her bath damp hair to her ankles. Alice was still serene as he fumbled with his trousers and spread her dancer's legs. Soft and yielding, moist too from the bath he kissed her dark flower. It was all sinking then, layer after layer of warm ice melting. They swayed to the rhythm of their squeaking glider.

—I love you, Alice. In her ear the voice whispered. Her breasts were wet, and a draft chilled them as it crawled up the side of her sweat dampened body away from Eddie's warmth. She had remained silent, forgotten the necessity of tears in the gentle rise and fall of her whole body as Eddie's hard hands worked beneath her buttock. But now a tear seemed to envelop her whole body. It was slick and drying cool where he had pressed down on her. It would freeze to something icy with sharp jagged edges. There would be between them this cold, brittle shell each time his maleness rose from her. Her body would always cry its tear of guilt, of shame, of bitter accusing anger. The emptiness could only have a name.

—Eddie, please get up. He rolled away, propping himself on his knee, his back against the sofa, one long leg stretching onto the floor. She gathered up the chenille robe, Mrs. Small's robe, and turning from him covered her dancer's body with pink. She spoke again, still with her back towards him, a slim column of pink crowned by dark, frazzled hair. You better go now, Eddie.

He was drained. Limp, deflated Eddie, boneless, pastel like a discarded balloon as he slid down onto the couch. Like sitting on the glass strewn ground Eddie felt, his bare ass rubbing against the tough fabric. He squirmed then conceded, melting without the strength to rise. —But, Alice, I love you.

Never turning, only pulling the robe righter as it rode up her dancer's calves, Alice spoke in the room of the dead Smalls, in the room where Brother slept, in the room she had left, in the room to which she had returned, in the love room, in the play room, in the room where the parade formed and the room where Eddie unable to stop her, dumbly regarded his wilted worm.

—Like Clara, Eddie, I gave it to you like Clara. A charity case free of charge on my lunch hour. We're the same now. I can tell her how gentle you are, how understanding. Please leave, Eddie, please get out of here! And don't come back! Please . . . please . . .

First one leg, then the other. It is a delicate balance really, especially when one knee trembles as the other is lifted. So loud sometimes, in this room like a train struggling through a tunnel as I push my foot through these trousers. The belt like a vice.

Where are they? One shoe shoved under the couch. There, I see it. When did I learn to make a bow. It seemed too hard at first. Automatic now, only difficult when I think about it. Alice's back. In spite of her voice I can see by her shoulders she is crying. Cry Alice, cry. Make Eddie cry. Look at Eddie cry. Cry Eddie, cry. Unbending from the task of shoe tying Eddie remained mute.

—Please, please get out. Docilely he shuffled towards the door. Her voice had broken, the second please a partial sigh. The pink shuddered.

I can't go, Alice. I love you Alice.

She hit him once, twice, sharp pummelling blows like a machine thudding on his shoulders and chest. The fury diminished, was finally crushed as he clasped her so tightly her clenched fists dug into her breasts. She struggled to free her arms, to release the terrible pressure his weight exerted on her pinioned elbows. Still fighting she was lifted flailing with one loose arm the steep sides of his boney, eggshell skull. She felt herself lurch as he lurched kicking at the bedroom door which burst open and tumbled them both sprawling onto her bed. He shook her naked body, his hands clamped around her wrists, shook her to a sitting position as his flushed face towered over her, the thick vein pulsating, his mouth working from which no words came. Straddling her he pushed her back onto the orange spread, pinning her wrists so she was powerless. Still her legs kicked futilely, and her head twisted from side to side. Then he was calm, strangely, frighteningly calm as he looked down on her nakedness, the heaving womanflesh stretched helpless in his grip. She lay suddenly motionless, her eyes widening as he stared down. She sensed his poised, inner stillness, the cold implacability of anything he decided to do. In that moment she loved him, loved the doom in his steel hands cutting into her wrists, the crushing, irresistible weight across her belly. Her lips were heavy with desire.

The black nipples, the thatch just beginning where I look

122

down, the dancer's legs, quiet now behind me, this flesh, this woman on a pink twisted cloud. Did I say I loved, did I shy away from her, did I take her in my hunger and my fear? My Alice. Is she this flesh?

It was all in his eyes, brown, deeply set. It was in every part of him touching her bare skin; he relaxed, the vein disappeared, the grief, the pain returned. Shy Eddie, averting his eyes, stepping down, like from a chair at the cookie jar and caught by his grandmother, stepping down, he backpedalled through the door, bowing almost to naked Alice who rose on one shoulder, hair wild. Softly behind him both doors closed.

It was still black, Eddie's time as he slipped through the dark streets. His sweat, her sweat, whatever else seeps out when people come together uncomfortable beneath his clothes. The fight with Mama, how had Alice known? Quickly, as his long legs stretched in faster, lengthened strides Alice was forgotten. Better to keep her as she was. Let her be like the music of the glider or their shrill singing and chants that were part of games. Rope skipping to the alphabet song. Spelling out your lover. Eddie, timid and frail, had played with the girls. But like the glider, all he could remember was a rhythm, the methodical repetition of rhyming words again and again. How did it go— Alice shouting, pigtails, braces, the thin knobby legs working like a pump, up-down, up-down as the rope swooshed over her head and flailed loud, dry bursts of dust from the pavement. Please Alice don't die. My turn soon, ducking under, knees bent, heart throbbing, straightening in stark terror of the fatal rope's snake touch.

But I must go back. There is nowhere else to go. He hoped his mother would be in bed. Sad Bette too he hoped. His little sister, and why did it have to happen to her? Life had touched his mother, made her old too soon. But there had been other things for her. She had been wife, mother, her years had been full. But Bette, what had she received? Eddie could not answer.

123

He felt the mist return to his eyes. Alice mist. Alice eyes. For a moment it had seemed that nothing wrong would ever happen again. After so long, Alice gliding beneath him, the love dance. Nothing now. Night now, streets strange and heavy sided, unfamiliar after just a year, a winding corridor thickly black that funnelled him to Dumferline Street where he turned towards home.

Bette waited in the livingroom.

—I'm so glad you're back. Bette paused reading her brother's eyes in the vestibule's dim light, Mama's asleep so shut the door quiet behind you.

Nothing ever changes thought Eddie, settling into the room's one soft chair. His sister was a blur, still standing one arm resting on the back of Mama's chair. Gentle, meek Bette, who if he asked would kneel down to bathe his feet.

—Want a glass of milk or something, Eddie? For her Eddie did wish there was something he wanted, something no matter how small she could do for him, something she could become for a moment that would draw her from the shadowed corner behind the chair.

—No, there's nothing I want now, but could you please turn on the light? It was hard to tell, but Eddie believed she had been crying. Her face was round, fuller than her mother's or Eddie's, more like the broad dimpled face of the dead father, Clarence. But nothing in it inclined towards excess, not his heavy jowls or stuffed cheeks, a completely female statement of his coarse good looks, softened, turned introspective and benign, a placid face even beautiful if caught in the correct light and in the particular repose unique to her kind of understated but perfect features. Unless the light was right her bad complexion would ruin the effect. A splotched, unhealthy type of skin, dark under her eyes.

—What's wrong, Bett? You look so sad.

—Nothing's wrong, nothing to speak of. I guess it's just my look. She looked so old sometimes, drab, loose housecoats down to her ankles almost, her head inclined slightly forward, a furrow in her brow, eyes that never met you, like the lids were too heavy to lift or the thick curled lashes stuck down. She seated herself, a weighty, resigned movement with nothing female in it; her hands settled into her lap.

—It's been a long time, Eddie, are you glad to be home? Mama and me sure missed you. Her voice rose and brightened as the sentence ended, as if word by word it entered her mind from a novel and unexpected source; she seemed surprised and gratified there was an echo returning the sound of her private thoughts.

—I missed you both, Bett, you'll never know how much. It was like I died or the world died, like nothing else existed, that I would never be able to get back home. I even began to believe home was something I had made up. Like the people we used to play with, like Mr. and Mrs. Booboo, remember, Bett? How we'd visit them and talk, and they'd take us places? I started to believe home was just make-believe like that.

—But you know we're real, Mama and me. I mean all the time you were away we were here, waiting and worrying. I prayed for you, Eddie, and Brother used to come around when Mama was asleep to talk to me. It was always about you. That Brother really remembers things. And he's so funny. I was always scared I'd burst out laughing and wake Mama. You know what a mess that would have been. Why doesn't she like Brother?

—Mama's sick Bett and she's getting old. I guess there are few things she still likes.

—It must be the worst thing in the world to be old. Old so you can't remember stories like Brother tells, or so old that the people you know best all begin dying. Do you think that's why Mama's so lonely? Bette's eyes dropped even lower. She rubbed the worn arms of her mother's chair slowly with both hands. —You know, Eddie, sometimes I feel like I'm getting old. When I'm here all day alone, with just Mama and that pup it's awful hard to remember other people, that maybe somewhere a radio might be playing or young people dancing, that there are shows and cars, and new clothes, and houses full of people laughing and talking together. I just have these walls, what you see around you, and Mama.

It was so easy to forget and Eddie felt ashamed because he had. Like a wet rag wiped over a spot, Alice gone, his love like Eugene's shoes left outside so it wouldn't contaminate the room. Only the itch in his groin, in the place he couldn't comfort while Bette sat watching in the room. Was everything so easy to forget, or was it his sister, this room where they had grown up together and the woman overhead asleep? Some special condition, as powerful and basic as *being Eddie,* which submerged all other considerations. Is this what it feels like to lose love, to sit and be sad because your sister is sad, to forget the object of that lost love so utterly that to think of her in this room is to feel awkwardness at the presence of a stranger? Have I returned for that?

—It's so good to have you home for Easter. Eddie started, suddenly, keenly aware of his sister's voice. Its tone, or a word, or just the nonverbal coincidence of some shade of his thought with that which produced Bette's utterance brought them into intimate contact again. Easter was when his grandfather had taken him to hear the sanctified people sing. Bette couldn't go because she was too young and Eugene couldn't be found so off they went, him perched on the old man's shoulder.

—Did you ever hear the saints sing? Bette smiled at her brother's question, her features relaxed and a secret light came from nowhere into her eyes.

—Remember big, fat Tiny, twinkletoes they called him. Brother must have told you stories if I haven't.

—Sure, I remember him being talked about, big as an elephant and black as coal.

—That was Tiny all right, but boy could that black elephant dance.

126

—Did you see him much? Bette began to lean forward excited, anticipating a story. Brother's talked about him, but not much. And I hardly remember the little he said. Just how he could dance. Bette knew the story from beginning to end, she had heard it rehearsed a thousand times in this same livingroom. But it had become a private, almost mystical link between brother and sister. An experience shared so deeply that its content had become superfluous; they could both fasten on the narrative and wring far more from it than any meaning translatable to an outsider. When Tiny danced, they moved into each other with the joy and fascination of lovers.

—Nothing like it, Bett. You've never seen nothing like it. He was round, huge and round with rolls of black fat. Always sweating, especially on his thick neck and his slick, light-bulb head. Like he had beads on sometimes, or shiny blisters sprouting all around his forehead and neck. He seemed to be crying when he danced cause the sweat poured down over his face, and he closed his little pig eyes to keep the salt out I guess, because if they weren't closed he squinted with a wrinkled-up, unhappy look on his face even though he danced and everybody knew he was happy. I sat on DaddyGene's shoulder and watched through a window. Talk about some colored people. Women with nets wrapped around the little, nappy hair they had, and the men sitting stiff in starched collars, like babies in high chairs with hard white bibs under their chins. But that was only until the music started. Everything—piano, trumpet, tambourines, drums, whatever anybody could beat or shake or blow noise through was in their hands and wagged at the devil. You think those Strip niggers can make a racket! Just go hear the sanctified one day.

Throughout Eddie's speech, Bette had been active, responding to each pause or gesture, squirming childishly in her seat to capture the essence of his words, the urgent masculine rhythms as his voice strained to keep pace with Tiny's dance. But as quickly as it came, it passed. Eddie's cheek dropped to rest on one clenched hand as if content to gaze thoughtfully and silently at a spectacle his words could no longer describe.

–Don't stop. Why are you stopping?

–Tiny's gone, Bett. For a minute Eddie could see him plainly, spinning like a shiny black top, faster and faster, close enough to touch, to hear it turning. Then he started to weaken, wobble, the heavy rolls around the middle dragging him down, he leaned just like a top leaning and spinning slower.

–Don't go away again Eddie, please don't go away again. There was a shriek in the night. First a stab of a yellow light against the tracks then diesel engines back to back rushed past. Eddie's lips moved instinctively, forming soft, reassuring words that if spoken would have been lost in the roar. When the clatter stopped these words had already died on his lips. He rose, moving hesitantly towards her chair, giving himself time to form others, to take advantage of the momentary reprieve forced upon him.

–Eddie . . . He was on his knees beside her before she could finish her sentence. Her moist eyes stared down at him full of fear, full of uncertainty and doubt. Could there be an answer? It was what her eyes asked . . .

–I must go away again. What I felt while I was away was the truth. There's nothing here for me. I'm dead, Bette, the plain fact of the matter is that Eddie's dead. You saw what happened when I tried to talk to Mama. If she saw me at all it was only on conditions that simply don't exist any more. If somehow I could return to her, return completely free of the past, if I could be a stranger, a kind stranger who reminded her of her lost son Eugene then she would accept me. But I can't be this—I've tried to erase my own past, but I can't do anything with hers, with all the long years we've shared . . . Mama can't forgive. Don't you see Bette? You too, you're a reminder of what she wants to forget. She manages to keep you from everything that could and should be yours. She's stealing it away bit by bit, and when there's nothing left she thinks things will be all right, she believes time will stop. That it will forget . . .

—What are you saying, Eddie, I don't understand.

—I'm saying you must get away from here, that I'm going away again, and this time you must go too.

—But Eddie, what about Mama, what will she do without me? You can't really mean what you're saying. You can't really say you want me to leave her alone in the world. She'd die, Eddie, she'd die right away without anyone to do for her, and it would be us that killed her.

—You're wrong, so, so wrong. A nurse could do for Mama. She's sick, and what she needs is a nurse.

—We don't have any money for that.

—We'll get money. That's the simplest thing. What's wearing Mama out is the two of us. She won't let go because it's only on us she can load her pain, and as long as we're close it's all she'll live to do. She'd be better dead, we'd be better dead.

There was a sharp tap on the stairs, another then the shuffling sequence of the old woman's stiff, braced legs lowered one at a time onto a step. Bette was on her feet and into the hall before Eddie could straighten up. Instantly he knew she had been listening, knew his words, finally stated, would bring his mother hurrying to confront him as fast as her withered body could move within the cold, steel bands. His limbs were leaden and morbidly sensitive at once. He felt enclosed in a warm, cloying liquid, the underwater torpitude of his nightmares suddenly remembered and real.

Bette switched on the light just as he entered the hallway. Blinking, shrinking from the light, his mother swayed at the top of the stairs, a ragged gray cloud just beginning to descend. Her eyes rolled wildly, her whole face contorted into something that could have been a mute's furious effort to scream. For a moment Eddie believed she had been stricken again, then as she raised the steel crutches menacingly to point or throw at him, it seemed she smiled, smiled because she knew he was trapped—for the split second she needed he was pinned to his tracks, an animal frozen under onrushing headlights. But the crutch never rose beyond her waist, and her lips stopped working to fall into a slack, idiot repose, as her eyes closed, and she pitched headlong down the stairs.

One look at the lifeless heap was enough. The dull robe discreetly shrouded her; only the metal poles protruded from beneath it and a dangling braid of grayish brown hair. A collapsed tent, with a bundle of sticks within rather than the soft, rounded contours of a human frame. Eddie burst through the front door, tearing into the night, but even as he ran and clamped his hands over his ears, Bette's scream and the puppy's banshee shrieks followed him.

In the street it all came back. Pursued, Eddie fled again through the dark corridor, the Furies writhing shapes his dogging shadow.

—What is your name, sir?

—Edward Lawson.

—Thank you, Mr. Lawson, and where do you live? Full address please.

—I don't have a full address, just a city.

—Family then, we must have next of kin, just in case.

—None.

—Well, is there anyone we can get in touch with Mr. Lawson, in case of some unforeseen difficulty or an emergency of some sort? This will all be kept private of course, and we don't expect to have to use the address you give us, but there is a certain form in these matters.

—Brother Small.

—Excuse me, is that a relative, a clergyman or . . .

—No, it's just a guy. A friend you can get in touch with—in case.

—Is that his complete name, or a title?

—Just Brother Small.

—Thank you, Mr. Lawson. And what's his address?

—The same as mine.

—Just a city?

—Yes.

—Thank you, just as you like, Mr. Lawson. You may go in to Dr. Grierson now. He's expecting you.

—Lawson, Edward . . . 30 . . . unemployed. I'm Dr. Grierson, Mr. Lawson. After a while here you'll probably find your own name for me, but for now Doc will be fine. Sit down, sit down please. These chairs are really quite comfortable, best ones on the whole reservation probably. I thought they'd be worth the extra expense if they'd induce people to come sit in them more than once coming in and once leaving. Nice aren't they? You won't find it as nice in your room. And there's a chance believe it or not that in time you may grow to hate your roommate more than you'll probably hate me. It's not that I'm a bad guy. It's simply that I'm the boss. The hands behind the stones that keep rolling up and down this bloody hillside. Are you a reader, Mr. Lawson? You have an intelligent eye. It says something here in your application about reading. What was it? Yes, hobbies: reading, painting. Fine, that's fine. We have books here, and we can get most any you want on loan from other libraries, and there's an arts and crafts shop. Maybe you'd like to work there. Nothing spectacular. At best stencil a few signs or make posters, probably wind up painting the dining hall. But perhaps something can be arranged. A mural perhaps. Scenes from the life of Christ or something. Well, I hope you like it here, Mr. Lawson. You won't at all, of course. It's miserable, it'll be a living hell, and if we weren't careful to keep the means out of hand most would slit their throats. But the point is there's no need. The gates are always open. Just check out with Mrs. West before you take off, if and when you decide to jump the reservation. She'll have a bunk for you now, and if someone is already there, try to have a little patience with whoever it is. In my experience it's always been so much easier if a chap can stick with one mate during his whole stay. Much better rate of rehabilitation, and often they leave quicker, sometimes even together. But that's far off. You'll have plenty of time on your hands so try to be patient with the other chaps. It helps everyone, especially us here in the office. You must come talk with me about your painting sometime, Mr. Lawson, or your reading. I like to be busy, and you'll learn the virtue of constructive activity here I'm sure. Mrs. West will arrange a schedule with you. Try you on a difficult one at first. See if you can handle it. From your reaction we can estimate something permanent. You'll receive treatments in the infirmary. Mrs. West has maps of the grounds and an orientation booklet. You'll find you'll have no difficulties at all in catching on. Just get along with your mate and be patient. It's part of yourself you have to find here, Mr. Lawson. All we can do here is restore you to yourself.

   –Saunders.
   –Lawson.
   –Just get in?
   –Yes. And you?
   –Four weeks, that's all, still a beginner.
   –Are you going to stay on?
   –Today, yes—I don't kid myself about tomorrow. I'll fight that battle when this one's off my hands. Where you from, Lawson?
   –East Coast.
   –Don't know anybody from out that way. I'm from Detroit myself, motor city.
   –Could you tell me which of these beds is yours?
   –The one beneath the window. I got my stuff spread all over the closet; I'll shove it to one side so you can put in your things. You get half the drawers too, but I hope you didn't bring too much. It's tight as hell already.

—I don't have much. Just some underwear and a shirt or two. For some reason I thought they'd have uniforms.

—There are overalls and workshirts you can borrow. Like this stuff in the closet here. They clean it free once a week in the laundry if you're interested. Most of the guys prefer street clothes. Cigarette, Lawson? Here, take a light too. I must smoke a million of these a day now, and if it's not one of these I got a chocolate stuck in my mouth.

—Chocolate?

—Yeah, ration of each. Chocolate and cigarettes. We get a couple of pounds of saltpetre a day in our food too. Ugh. Somebody should tell the management that most of the poor studs here don't even remember it's for something besides pissing, let alone care. That's right, plop right down. Your place too now. I gotta take a little stroll for a couple of minutes. Make yourself at home, and if there's anything I can help you with, just ask. It takes some settling in, man, Papa Grierson undoubtedly let you know just how hard it is. Some guy. Pisses everybody off the first time, but he ain't so cool really, just a pill-pusher, pushing a funny kind of pill. Kinda guy you just avoid, loves to hear himself talk. Get to know the other fellows, don't cross anybody and you have a fifty-fifty chance of being a winner. That big room of Grierson's is just a place to get in trouble. Well, I gotta go. See you later Lawson.

—Lawson?

—Yeah, Saunders.

—You know I was just thinking. Wonder why I still call you Lawson and you call me Saunders.

—It's what we called each other the first day.

—But it ain't quite right, is it, Lawson? I mean after people know each other a while they start using other names.

—I'd feel funny calling you anything besides Saunders. Calling you Ron, or Ronald would be strange for me. You're Saunders.

—And you're Lawson. That's the sort of conclusion I came to myself. But it made me think of something else too. It's hard to explain, but you got a good head, Lawson, maybe you can even help me say it.

—Words are not my department.

—I know, but it's not words that I need. It's something else. Did you ever go to church, Lawson? I ain't asking that to be personal, I mean I don't care which one, or how long ago, or anything like that. In fact, I ain't a believer myself. But I did go to church, long ago when I was a boy. With my mother mostly, and sometimes she'd cry and get the old man to go too. But have you been, Lawson?

—When I was a kid.

—That's enough; you'll understand. Well in my church, when the preacher was talking, and he said something really fine, something that everybody understood or that plopped right into the guts of one of the shouting members of the congregation, out would come a loud *Amen*. *Amen* Lawson, you know what I mean, do you remember *Amen?* It was like, like, hell, I can't explain it, but if you remember hearing people say *Amen,* loud and clear, with their faces shining, almost laughing it seemed a lot of the time, then you know the kind of help you can give me with what I want to say.

—Are you going to preach me a sermon?

—C'mon Lawson, you know what I'm trying to get at. What I wanted to say in the first place was things about this place really scare the shit out of me sometimes.

—Amen.

—Wait a minute now. I got more to say than that. The bit about names is what started me thinking. Here I am. One day you just walk in and say you're going to be living with me. O.K., that's simple enough, I don't know nothing about nothing, where you came from, what you do, your name even, and in lots of ways that's good. It's good cause it's so different from

134

out there. I meet a stud here and we're really just two, plain studs. Nobody got nothing going. I meet a stud here and all's I know is that we have the same kick and we're both trying to shake it. Now if you see what I mean, that's good, it's clean, I mean everybody really has a clean slate here. You start over again, like being a baby again or something. But this ain't really the world is it? I mean we're on a kind of island, or in a jail almost. So you call me Saunders and I call you Lawson. It's what we did first, so that's what sticks, that's what's O.K. It don't matter who you are or who I am, Lawson and Saunders is enough. But when I leave here, I ain't Saunders no more. You remember a stud named Saunders, but as soon as I walk through that gate, he dies. Maybe something real good happened to Saunders, maybe Saunders is even straight. But what about the poor bastard walking down that hillside? What good will Saunders do me, huh, what good will all this shit do me on the other side?

—Still hanging on, Lawson?
—Yessir.
—Did you get a good roomie?
—Yessir, but he left last week.
—Oh yes, that's right . . . Saunders, he didn't even warn us beforehand. He was very, very grateful. I remember now, he mentioned you. Yes, I recall it all quite clearly. Mrs. West was quite impressed. She remarked on the change in his attitude, how he seemed even physically transformed, years younger. I think he could have gotten a date, Lawson. She's not bad you know. Just a poor dresser. Good strong legs. He'll have another chance I bet. That is if he fights back at all. He was kidding himself. Look Lawson, I'm going to drop by and see you some day soon. You won't mind, will you? I promise I'll be stimulating. Perhaps we could talk about your painting or your reading. Find yourself another friend. It really helps. And above all don't

brood on Saunders, neither on his absence nor his presence out there. You'll need all the strength you have to keep yourself above water.

Sept 4

Hello Brother:

It's raining like hell here. I don't expect you anymore, but that's something you had to decide for yourself. The fellow I wrote to you about before—Saunders—returned last week and looks pretty bad. He doesn't want to room with me again. Shame can do terrible things to a man; I could feel the pain it caused him when I tried to approach. His hurt is like a bell, something I can hear when he walks past at night. Sometimes I believe it wakes me up. Twice I've found myself wide awake, sitting up in bed in the middle of the night. And both times it was him prowling around when he believes no one sees him. I wonder if anyone else can hear it. Sometimes I wonder if I'm not nuts. The thing that frightens me most is that if I am crazy, I have to stay that way, and even get crazier to ever leave this place.

Dec. 12

Dear Alice, . . . Dear Alice, . . . Dear Alice, . . . Dear Alice, . . . Dear Alice, . . . Dear Alice, . . . Dear Alice, . . . Dear Alice, . . . Dear Alice, . . .

—You learn quickly, Eddie. If I believed in naturals, I'd say you were one. You really feel you wouldn't want to stay on? Not even with the prospect of possibly defeating me one fine day as incentive? I took you for the dedicated, intense type. Not a plodder, by any means, don't think I'm that insensitive to character, I rather intend a compliment to your scrupulous perseverance. The key word is of course scrupulous with its moral connotations and the meticulous solicitude and judgment it involves. I could see you performing many of the most difficult tasks of a civilization. Purifying the language of the tribe so to speak, or its vision, or perhaps something as basic as refining the very heart of the multitude. But now I'm waxing romantic. Chess is an interesting game, ancient and interesting, Eddie. This very set we're using has it's personal history, a long line of ancestors from whom it has received the substance of these final rarified and abstracted forms. What do you think about ancestors, Eddie? How far back can you trace your family, are there any traditions passed down through the male line which the men in your family relish as a sacred trust? It was originally an Eastern game. And in essense it remains oriental, doesn't it? The miniature delicacy and virtuosity that can be displayed in the carved figures, the immutability of the checkered board itself and the rigidity of the movements each piece can perform. Finally, the deliberate rhythmic changes in the disposition of each player's force over which the master's face broods serene. At times the moon, at times the waves. There is a particular beauty when the master resigns himself to the will of the carved jade, wood or ivory. Two minds working furiously, fiercely antagonistic, veiled, subdued, yet all spirit, the dross refined away by rules, by the convention of these little figurines sliding from square to square. Only two words needed and with these two words we can express completely the intricate twisting and turnings of minds engaged, of minds truely communicating. Not the feeble monosyllable *love,* not what the ostriches continue to squeal in spite of thousands of years of disappointment and frustration. That empty signal is forsaken. We move in the eternal dance of *Check,* Edward, and *Check-mate.*

Mar. 27

Dear Mama and Bette:

I will be coming home soon. That's all I can say now, but in a way one of the reasons I'm returning is because at last I feel I have something to tell you. It's a strange world here, suffering and pain everywhere. At any time of the day or night you can hear the screaming of grown men; wild screams like babies crying till they almost choke. You hear men crying like that, and you begin to be afraid that the sound is really part of breathing. That if one stops, the other will, and a man must die. Mama, I'll need your help when I return. I learned a man can only do so much alone, that he has to grab onto something outside himself, whether it be a good thing or a bad one. Deep inside there is only screaming, that or a dull, smothering silence. After we reach that deep, the only hope is to see a hand, or hear a quiet voice, anything outside that can be believed, that is as real as the madness. They put Saunders on a train; some of us accompanied the hearse to the depot. His sister will meet the body in Detroit. You never realize how helpless you are till you see pain in another person's eyes.

But from all this I'm coming home. I'll see you soon Mama, and you Bette, and Brother. You can't believe what strange things come into my mind when I try to think of you all, how in funny ways I can't remember the simplest things. But the winter's over, it's already becoming warm enough for shirt sleeves here, and I hope to be with you to celebrate Easter.

Easter and home. Eddie's chest was full. Burning phlegm congested his throat and lungs; the horrible sounds of the day padded his brain with clumps of thorn bushes. Tioga Street Sanctified in the Name of Jesus Christ Church. Eddie entered and sat near the back, behind a few scattered faithful still unredeemed who waited even unto this late hour for a sign. No lights were on. Only a brace of stumpy candles glowered in one corner, shuddering uneasily in the draft, almost audible like a frightened child's murmurs in the darkness. Eddie wondered which saints were there or who sat alone like he did on a saint's hard bench.

Outside the street was quiet; no traffic sounds and only an infrequent footfall rising then gone in a dying fall, the single, lazy motion of a swing. Eddie wept. In the dark interior alone in his corner nothing seemed more natural. His lament completed a vague symphony he had been creating unaware during the entire day. One by one the themes had first stirred into life, Brother, Mama, Alice, brief, bright flames kindled from the

138

embers Eddie's breath heated, then waning again to ashes that burned acrid in his nostrils and stuck in his throat.

The loud rattle of newspaper unfolded broke into Eddie's thoughts. His eyes, grown accustomed to the darkness, discerned a shape at the end of his bench, a man's huddled figure materializing out of the gloom as if created by Eddie's sharpened perception.

—Piece of bread young man? Eddie was startled. The man had been there all along, all through Eddie's utter submission to grief. A witness authenticated by his gravelly voiced offer of a crust of bread, a witness mocking. Eddie was not aware of how long he sat under the sway of his thoughts, apparently oblivious to the other's sudden appearance. He was shocked and helpless on the bench's edge; his eyes fixed on the apparition as if to keep it real and tangible till the flurry of other thoughts passed, and his mind and voice would be his own.

—I'll keep my bread then, mister. Nobody asked you to sit on my bench. You ain't a sanctified I know. By now the stranger's voice had risen above the original hissing undertone in which he had summoned Eddie's attention. To Eddie he seemed to be shouting in the silence of the sanctuary. Eddie knew the few saints would be staring with shock and outrage at this encroaching corner.

—Please, please be quiet.

—Quiet, who the hell are you telling to be quiet. I listened to your bawling and didn't complain. All the time hungry, but waiting till you finished before I opened my bread. Who do you think you are mister! The man was shouting. Eddie could see him more clearly now, a grizzled old man in an ancient oversize army coat that gave him an enormous floundering indefiniteness in the obscurity of the narrow aisles. The loose bench grated as he arose and stumbled towards the door. As he passed Eddie a wave of heat and pungent wine rottenness enveloped the young man.

—Go to hell you sorry-assed, ungrateful bastard, the derelict shouted from the entrance. All you fools will be in a box soon enough, just like that stiff up there in his waiting for some goddamn angel to come and carry him away. Like grotesque snowflakes they sailed and landed silently, the slices of bread he tossed into the store-front church. The saints near the front began to moan in superstitious awe of this blaspheming vision. A bent woman in black scrambled awkwardly from her seat to kneel before the coffin resting in front of the makeshift altar. As a laugh and more curses thundered from the doorway she rose with a scuttling crab urgency, huddling protectively her thin frame over the smooth wooden box.

—Jesus, Jesus, help me Jesus, the few saints bleated in a confused chorus to drown out the mad laughter. Eddie watched numb, petrified till the wino had gone and the saints' frightened prayers subsided. Why so heavy Brother, why does he try to lift such heavy ones? Eddie watched as they struck harmlessly far down the hillside, why such heavy ones?

The saints had moved closer together. Five or six mourners humming in subdued melodious voices.

Eddie wished for something as solid as the rhythm and words of a hymn. Something which would draw him into the confiding, mellow harmony which the saints shared, something to drive away fear and death from the darkness.

Nearer my God to thee, nearer, nearer to thee, he recognized it of course, even in the monolithic, languishing cadences of the saints. Each note was something they dwelled upon, something tasted and savored, a tangible joy he knew was there but whose substance was lost to him. He could at most recall the joy as a powerful presence—sometimes sweet, sometimes threatening, a presence which had promised him even vaster and more mysterious possibilities as he sat a child in the church. That promise had once burned. Could be taken blissfully into his whole being as once the nipple and cloud of flesh resting on his lips.

140

To touch the hem of his garment, Eddie closed his eyes, settling into the deeper darkness as he bowed his head. Alice the dancer. The stickiness in his groin had begun to itch again. Flowing from her buttock, the pure, untasted excess of their coming together. Gone to itchiness in his body hair. In this chaste vault with angels singing Eddie scratched because he was alone. Eddie followed in his mind and even to the edge of his lips the hymn they were singing. From his saint's bench he leaned to retrieve the heel of bread hurled in anger by the wino. Pure, untasted. Eddie tore off a piece, compressing its substance in his hands. The ball he formed was moist from the sweat of his palms. He broke it with his teeth into two soft hemispheres. It had been almost perfectly round, and wetting both halves with his tongue he reformed the globe then hungrily chewed it. The wino's laugh returned. The stones bounding down the hillside, Alice so warm beneath his hands, the old woman from the top crashing. She would not taste again, never even this, even the staleness of this crust consumed while the saints sing.

Nearer, nearer to thee.

Eddie rose, turning his back on it all. The candles were nearly dead, but whistling louder to him than the saints' drone. In the street their paltry light was a glare, then nothing as he blinked away their image.

Thurley was drunk, drunk and floundering as he and Al entered the chapel. Al, just as high, had never stopped talking as the two men wove their way through the ivy covered American Gothic buildings of the campus, the scenic route from Al's bungalow to the chapel, and Thurley had been reminded of his alma mater quickly and lost himself in sentimental reveries to which Al's almost angry voice was an insistent counterpoint. Somewhere along the way Al had become lost and confused. Their perambulation came to a lurching, unsteady stop beside an undergraduate residence hall.

—It says Potter over the door, Al.

—Potter, yes. Potter. Named for Israel Potter, hero of Melville's romance. But not really Bob, it's some rich founding father, probably one of your New England respectables I'd venture to say. A fine Anglo-Saxon name Potter, and Potter is just seconds away from our destination.

Just beyond the far corner of the tile roofed building the turf was cut by a narrow gravel walk that curved gracefully out of sight again behind another series of stone dormitories on slightly higher ground. Over this cluster of dull red roofs a steeple climbed into view.

—You understand now, Bob, this is not the real thing at all. Just massed choirs, and a good professional priest singing parts of the Mass. But you get the effect anyway. Most of the hymns we'll hear will be in fact processionals, what the Greeks sing parading through the little village streets on Good Friday behind the icons and candles, but I think they'll come off inside. If we're lucky we can sit close. I like to watch the faces. Especially the kids if there are any. Children singing is one of the few things I still believe in, Bob. Have you ever watched them? My first Easter in Greece it was all I could do to keep from hugging every scrubbed little body. Everyone's in the street. They wait for midnight and the Papa to come bursting from inside the church. *Krystos Anesti*—he shouts beaming from beard to bun. He mounts a little raised platform outside the church and around him, illumined by rows of candles or a spotlight if one's available, the most holy objects are gathered. *Krystos Anesti*—he shouts and the crowds respond—*Alithos Anesti*—truly, truly risen. Oh, Bob, if you could have seen the children. Each face lit up by its own glowing candle. The dark eyes wide and excited. All around maniacs shooting off firecrackers, in your ears it seems, the sky filled with these great swan dives of bursting colors. You have to see it, Bob. We'll go together someday; we'll climb Lycabettus together and be part of the fiery snake slinking down its sides.

If Thurley had been sober, he would have been embarrassed

by the volume of Al's voice still loud as they found seats in the chapel. As it was he smiled inwardly, happy because Al seemed happy, and the smoke from burning incense rising in the church's transept became for him the exhaust of fire bombs shot off and echoing in the vastness of the distant vaulted arch. Simultaneous with a shush from an annoyed spectator, the solemn drone of a rich bass voice issued from the dazzling altar temporarily valanced with ornate cloth of gold drapery. The shuffle of feet moving to a lugubrious cadence began behind them. A female chorus in long, dark dresses, topped by tunics of white and gold, marched towards the cramped wooden benches of the choir loft beside the bearded priest. Others followed till the cantor was surrounded by a brilliant patchwork of gilt and color. A priest robed in white swung a thurible hypnotically in front of the altar while two small boys, their faces made pale by glowing surplices, passed up and down the side aisles waving their antique copper dishes of incense suspended from chains. Wisps of scented smoke floated in the chapel's dark, drafty insides. The voices of the combined choirs began as a rumble, but quickly dissipated in the corners and recesses of the intricate Gothic interior. The music seemed to flee, to hide, to become lost; it wandered ghostly and was trapped in the dark covered ambulatory, it was exhausted, rising up past the triforium into the rarefied, blazing air of the clearstory where shafts of sunlight smoked. Thurley followed it, his ear inordinately keen, listening to the melancholy plash of music against ungiving stone. Al had become deadly silent, as if he too was constrained to share the music's fate.

A solo woman's voice began a long, aching lament. When she reached the uppermost registers her magnificent control never faltered, the rich tones were undiminished, instead they radiated like a fountain at its peak shimmering into crystal spray indistinguishable from the atmosphere in which it danced. Her song created an unbearable tension throughout the audience. Thurley knew it was an act of pure will, a strenuous exertion of forces within himself he only reluctantly brought to bear, which kept him seated. The woman's solo was too perfect, it arched too highly, even beyond the thick joints of the groined ceiling, and if nothing else, if the effort did not bring the singer crashing down, then at last the song itself would end, and Thurley must plunge from its heights. He experienced an uncanny prescience; he didn't need to look around to know that the others were rapt in fear and submission, to know that Al sat weeping beside him, the tattered remains of his program forlorn in his lap. Thurley knew he must leave, knew he must escape the siren song of her perfect voice foraging like a hungry beast among the stones inside the chests of the audience. Something welled up in his stomach. At first he feared it was a scream, an irresistible ear-splitting scream that would suck away his life's breath as it tore from his body. Then he knew it was sickness. Sour tasting, animal sickness as he stifled a belch, and the fumes rose to coat his throat. Al never noticed him get up, in fact every eye was fixed on the singer as Thurley fled from his seat and hurried giddily on tiptoe up the aisle.

He was barely outside before he doubled up, lunging towards a tree against which he shot out a stiffened arm for support. The gin of an afternoon splattered against the tree's gnarled roots and flecked the thick soles and sides of his cordovans. When he raised his head, he noticed clouds. Deep, gray clouds from nowhere piling up in ranks to obscure the blue sky. No one in sight. Al's voice gone, the priest gone, the woman gone, the choirs and sweet, drifting incense gone. Thurley wiped his mouth. He knelt down and brushed the vomit from his wing-tipped shoes, discarding the soiled sudarium as he arose. A light snowlike shower of blossoms was falling around him. He looked down at his feet and saw the fluttering mounds these tiny petals had formed drifting apart, silently scattered as the breeze curled among them. Although the clouds moved rapidly and short gusts of wind agitated the blossoms, a dead, still calm engulfed Thurley.

The foliage of enormous horse chestnut trees forming a grove around the chapel swayed and rustled, one tree in particular, its shaggy outline flocculent against the dulling sky trembled as the wind's invisible hand dug deeply into its branches. The blanched undersides of its leaves flapped and quivered into view, conical bunches of flowers swayed then released a rain of white petals. Enveloped in his own stillness Thurley saw it all frighteningly accelerated, like a motion picture flickering at the wrong speed, the scene around him became poignant simply because it unfolded too quickly to follow. He felt suddenly weary, suddenly weak and old. There was no way to catch up, no way to remove himself from the unnatural calm. He saw faces looking down on him, grief-stricken, pitying faces obscured by veils. Thurley was stiff and unmoving; the faces passed in procession peering down from a tremendous height, each one tendering only a brief pathetic glance, as if afraid a longer look would draw them into the pit where Thurley was stretched cold, unmoving as stone. Thurley wanted to feel the wind, wanted it to lap inside his clothes and finger his body. The blossoms swam by his eyes. Jerky, uneven movements as they circled closer to the earth. Shuddering it seemed as a puff of air shot them forward, then suddenly dropped its support. It would rain soon, and the puddles would be thick with white blossoms. They would float, mixing with the scum and acrid green to form mottled rainbows in stagnant pools. The air brought its message of rain in a cool draft across Thurley's perspiring face. As he walked, clouds clustered around the sun, and long tree shadows disappeared insensibly into the general darkness.

THREE

The powerful engine revving beneath him brought no relief. Thurley drove like a madman, but the faster the automobile sped along route seventy-two, the deeper into a black, yawning gulf it seemed to carry him.

A queasy after-sickness was all that remained of the gin's euphoria; a vitus dance of thought replaced his sensual apprehension of the afternoon's events. He recognized the increasingly morbid content of these thoughts as the black winged drones of a sweeping depression he knew he had no strength to resist. He had to find a room, a room swarming with other men, a dark, whiskey perfumed place where the spirit could drown without thrashing and gasping for breath.

After mounting the stairs, Thurley's progress was impeded by a thick, metal door, and he stood on Harry's bright threshold ill at ease beneath a single, naked bulb. He knew he was being watched, silently appraised through a narrow slit of one-way glass by Ollie, the one-eyed, antediluvian doorman who never forgot a face. As he stood aside, his wizened body straining to hold the door, Ollie screwed the death mask of his features into its customary grimace of greeting which by convention passed for a smile among the frequenters of Harry's Place. Thurley was no stranger to the old black man and his fifty-cent piece dropping with a solid ring into Ollie's white saucer was an ornament left as incentive to other customers but seldom matched between his visits. This model gratuity brought both Ollie's crooked yellow teeth into view and earned the subtle compliance of his bow. With alacrity he depressed a hidden buzzer summoning the steward to a second portal further down the fuliginous corridor. Another pair of heavy doors swung mystically inward, emitting a gust of clotted music and laughter that floated down the dusty hall dying before it reached Ollie's table, chair and porcelain nest crowded by the silver coin. Thurley was inside.

Sunday was the biggest day for Harry's Place. The state's obsolete blue laws which made after hour joints financially practical also added those inestimable second relishes of sin and secrecy, and Harry kept it close to pitch dark so his clientele could savor these virtues. In every corner of Harry's, people felt they were getting away with something. Occasionally to heighten the aura of authority flaunted there were well advertised police raids, usually on odd Mondays when a few paid stooges and forgetful winos were ceremoniously packed into paddy wagons and hauled away. Everybody knew Harry did it that way just to keep the heat off, and to further demonstrate his power over the *man,* the club's bouncer was always a uniformed cop. Thurley was one of few white customers. The reason for this aside from the fact Harry's was deep in the Strip was the women. Although available in various degrees, they were not professionals and a certain fierce etiquette protected them from all white prowlers and Negroes not prepared to go through preliminary gallantries no matter how brief or coarse. The kind of woman who came, the sister, aunt, cousin, neighbor, or even mother of the men, made this code necessary and brutally enforced. Trespasses against it caused most of the incidents in or outside Harry's. Thurley smoothing his way in with heavy tipping and discretion, became a sort of unobtrusive fixture on weekends. One or two white faces could be seen among a hundred or so other customers most busy nights, but they were always the same. Thurley had never approached any of these other white men and gradually had subdued his curiosity about their motives. He valued too much the special kind of peace that allowed him to effectively sink his identity into the darkness of Harry's Place. Always the same bartender, the same stool, the same drink that never had to be ordered. He was simply Bob to the few people who spoke to him, and neither he nor anyone else wanted more.

The weekend band was playing, a local group whose special talent was making a racket loud enough to be heard over the general din. It was always hot in Harry's, and the band leader wore a sweat band around his head. Above it in deep greasy swirls, Indian Slick's processed hair was plastered to his skull.

Indian Slick had a way of moving which disturbed Thurley. After each number, keeping his elongated torso rigid on the piano stool, and his thin arms, bent at the elbow and wrist, suspended over the keyboard, he would twist his head around on the column of his skinny neck to study the audience through grotesquely outsized sunglasses. Something about this praying mantis posture, the frozen intentness of the little Negro at the piano had made Thurley wary from his first encounter with it. When the band broke up for a short intermission Slick joined Thurley at the bar.

–Little word to the wise on this happy Easter day my friend. Let me buy you a drink too, and I'll have one whiles we talk this little matter over. The bartender moved opposite Thurley and his sudden host, immediately acting on the signal for drinks from Slick. As soon as they were set down, Slick raised his glass to his mouth. He sipped slowly, never moving the glass from his lips, gradually tilting the vessel till its contents had been drained. When he finished he began speaking again, taking for granted he had retained Thurley's attention although a space of several minutes had elapsed, and his absorption in this peculiar intaking of liquor made it obvious he was no more concerned with the people around him than an aphid milking a plant.

–You know Brother Small, don't you? Nice fellow, Brother. But Brother got a friend certain people around here don't like, and they have good reason believe me. These people thought you might be able to speak to Brother. Tell him just to stay away from this fellow he thinks is his friend. Brother'll know who you mean; he's been shooting his mouth off about how his friend would be back for Easter. But if he acts dumb, you just say Eddie Lawson, tell Brother we mean he should keep clear of Eddie Lawson and keep Eddie outta here. Now you're Brother's friend and these people think he'll listen to you. I mean nobody's involving you in anything, you can tell him or not, it's up to you, and they don't care if you do or if you don't, they just thought you might drop him a little word to the wise, from the wise. It might save him some bad trouble and I thought you'd like to help him, you being his friend and all that.

—Eddie, Eddie Lawson.

—That's the name. You know 'em?

—Brother just mentioned him once or twice.

—Just take my word friend, Lawson is pure trouble, and Brother's asking for it if he hangs around 'em. Just a word to the wise of course. Now I got to go back to work, friend.

Thurley was sweating. He reached into the inner pocket of his light suit jacket feeling for a handkerchief. His hand met the square corners of a folded piece of paper. He drew it out, forgetting in his curiosity the dampness of his forehead and at the back of his neck. It was a program from the cathedral, a single white sheet folded in half so it gave the contents of four consecutive Sunday musicales. The Easter extravaganza was announced on the first page. Thurley turned it over quickly, ignoring its numerous credits in small print, list of choirs, soloists and the orthodox hymns in Greek characters with translations bracketed beneath. On the third page, after running through the usual introduction preceding the music titles, Thurley's eyes were riveted to the program. Unbelievingly, softly aloud he read *A Cantata, The Voices of Children, by Professor Al Levine, Head of the College Music Department. This new work, directed by the composer, will receive its initial performance.* Al's secret, why he could smile.

Thurley knew in an instinctive flood of confidence that the

music would be grand, would express Al's tremendous talent, his energy and meticulous craftsmanship. But then after a moment's consideration, although he still believed it would be good, Thurley realized good or bad didn't matter most; the point was that Al could stand in front of them safe for a moment, pure as he lifted his arms and began to direct the chorus. In that moment free, the past erased, no past except what was focused upon and consumed in the first swell of singing voices. Soft, fluttering Al at rest, at peace, something that to Thurley always seemed impossible to achieve for himself or anyone else—till it happened. A cantata, a poem, a book, they meant nothing in themselves, anything could be the reason to rise up high. Thurley knew too well the illusion of completion, the crazy idea that the chase really ends. How empty, how desolate the disenchantment could be. Thurley knew he would never willingly be born again, never be a child if one condition was remembering this backside of experience which two thirds of a lifetime thrust in his face. But each time he lifted a pencil or turned a page, this knowledge was a weight on his chest; it strained every sinew of his will to shake free from the taunts and laughter, from the certainty of failure his first step assured. A poem, a book. Too big for the narrow pinnacle, they must topple from the summit to the very depths, and the same inescapable logic that put a man behind a stone drew him after it in its fall. Thurley saw Al loinclothed, his small, perfect limbs toiling. Al Sisyphus reaches the top, balances one precarious second, smiling in the glare of brilliant flashbulbs as angels crowd to take his picture. Al beautiful, poised, with a verve that seems will sustain him however, fig-leafed Al and the depths beneath.

Thurley found his handkerchief. He also replaced the program tenderly inside his coat. He was smiling to himself, the absurdity of his vision, little Al naked, struggling with a boulder up a steep rise was just too incongruous with the immaculate, be-Dacroned back he knew Al would present to the audience as he turned towards his singers. Even funnier was the thought of his own red flesh quivering in the same task. I would need two fig leaves in the garden. Because that's where it began; wasn't innocence just the first way station at the foot of the slope, a place to refresh, to grab a drink before starting up? Certainly nobody could stay there, nobody would want to if they had eyes and a brain, and as long as these continued to function there could be no true desire to return, just moments of utter fatigue when another drink is needed. Once past it, the wish can only be in terms of choosing life or death, to stop or go on. The poem becomes an oasis, a sort of gas station that is only sought because it provides the means of going on, not a destination . . . *an old man in a dry month, Being read to by a boy,* for some reason, as they often did, the lines came to Thurley. They broke into the mild self-satisfaction he felt with his gas station metaphor. Eliot was for him the poet of weariness, of old age. His frightened old men had aged the undergraduate Thurley prematurely, and strangely, they now came back bringing Thurley a poignant feeling for youth. It had all gone so quickly. Between two readings of a poem his lifetime had nearly slipped away. Sometimes it seemed like that. That only a few events, insignificant on any objective scale but emotionally charged beyond calculation had been crowded into a morning and afternoon, a poignantly recent time, so close it seemed that now as he sat in a long evening of recollection something still could be done. But he knew once gone was always gone, time past had no minutes or years. In fact it seemed colors were much more adequate to describe his fast receding day, blues, reds, yellows, violets, a glowing spectrum from blazing white to the black of night.

Thurley spoke silently to Al. But we are not old men. You proved you had further to go, wanted me to hear it and see it. In a way another's triumph can be just as refreshing as my own, but since I'm selfish and weak, it's just as likely to bring pain before its full meaning penetrates. Like the woman's voice this afternoon. I couldn't keep it down, how could I sit still in the presence of beauty knowing what I do. But with you it's different, and your cantata will be beautiful, it must be beautiful, and I will come to hear it. I will not be afraid, and I won't torment myself with the illusion that such beauty only comes from beauty and is only for the beautiful. That's what makes the music of strangers so exquisite, what often makes it unbearable. It seems to come from nowhere, to be pure and unattainable. It seems to somehow make a link with what I've been clumsily seeking and by the perfection of this link seems to exhaust the source. But it isn't like that. It's dirty business, sweating, bitter work, like you've done, Al, like I must continue doing. Strange how wrestling with angels makes us so dirty. You'd think they'd smell of perfume, be soft and clean. But it's you struggling up the hill I'll remember, Al, you with your perfect buttocks and legs straining like they did that night with Eleanor, that I will believe in.

Al disappeared, his familiar face melting again into the noise and darkness of the bar. They had been speaking, he must have been with Al; the words had been important to Thurley, and Al's face had been so close and intent as he listened. Thurley wanted the handsome face and dark eyes again, wanted to express his sincerity in a long, direct look Al would be sure to understand. He must know I meant every word, even down to the bold *I will not be afraid.* How long since I've said that to myself. It's a child's phrase, something said to goblins, to wild animals, to mothers, to other little boys and especially to myself in empty rooms at night with their lights extinguished. Am I really not afraid? What Indian Slick said to me is not to be disregarded or taken lightly. I've been around long enough to recognize the unquestionable authority of some people's words to the wise. Also, another wouldn't have been involved, especially a white man unless something serious was concerned. Brother Small. The name called up no definite response in Thurley's mind. The one outstanding fact about his frequent house guest was the one first surmounted and forgotten by Thurley—Brother's unrelieved albino ugliness. After that Thurley realized he could recall very little. Aside from Brother's pell-mell monologues only partially understood by Thurley, they had no conversations. Brother never seemed to listen to whole sentences. Disregarding the direction and even content of Thurley's speech, except in the simplest question or command, Brother responded according to a logic only he understood. Certain words no matter what their context, and ideas only loosely associated with Thurley's meaning were what he seemed to reply to. Clustered around certain words like *Eddie* there was an endless constellation of incidents which Brother dramatized in his original but disconcerting manner. But by frequently sounding this particular signal, Thurley had gained a familiarity with Eddie at once intimate and mysterious. The intensity of their only meeting had given a spur more than curiosity to Thurley's interest. In a life he felt was shrunken to a minimal content of event and emotion, that rare evening had haunted him, the violence of the young man pinned Thurley down, defined him in heavy strokes as relentlessly accurate as the beauty of the woman's voice.

There had been a Thurley where Eddie saw one. A hungry, preying animal only barely concealed beneath his clothes. But there was more, something Thurley now felt impelled to make clear although he had failed so many times before. Perhaps Al already knew, could already understand, and if he hadn't heard Thurley speak, then after Al's music when they talked again, Thurley would repeat what he had said. But how could Eddie know that beneath his olive suit, within the flushed, white flesh was a consciousness just as acute, just as accusing, just as aware of the beast as Eddie's hate had made him. And if they could meet so powerfully, if the same anger could be shared, could not remorse and the act of forgiveness bind them just as tightly? In this desire to share, to submit to someone else's judgment what he thought he had learned about himself, truth as far as an active, unremitting search had revealed it, Thurley had always been held back by fear. And as long as this fear remained he had to flee.

As he became aware of the music again, Thurley noticed his drink sat still untouched. Around him the shadowy forms of the Negroes like dark, inverted ghosts were absorbed into the narcotic clamor. He stood alone, voluminously robed in a brilliant arc of light, his arms gloved in crimson from the limp fingertips to the elbows. At his feet, supine between the pavement and gutter, the slaughtered offering laved the stones from hidden wounds. A mist rose from the corpse, like cigarette smoke at first, then thickening, congealing to a weighty death's head floating above it. It was a skull, then a full bearded tragic mask in flowing headdress. Slowly the horror began to fade from its eyes, the deeply cut furrows of tension softened and eased, the mouth relaxed its half gulping, half screaming downward slant, the face became younger, the mild, wondering gaze of a youth mortally stricken, the simultaneous disbelief and disillusion Thurley knew was Eddie's face beneath the lamp.

They passed within three yards of him, the albino and the slim figure of his bowed friend, like one body as they slipped through the mass of dark, oblivious jelly. A single blues chord crashed from the piano and was repeated with monomaniacal persistence like a lunatic dashing his head against the ground. The sound increased in intensity till it seemed the blows were struck by feet rather than hands, by someone possessed who jumped up and down with ragged precision to annihilate some doomed section of the keyboard. Like carrion crows towards a death smell a crowd gathered around Indian Slick. Four or five couples streaming with sweat still gyrated on the dance floor. They had given over all semblance of form, submitting to the primitive, insistent force of the music. The couples disintegrated into single, unapproachable entities. Each dancer seemed to be fighting a desperate internal battle, contorting every limb, every joint, pushing his body to an excess and exaggeration of every sense, outraging its reluctant, lethargic core, as if instinctively grasping pure outrage was the only kind of arousal that would raise him to the pitch of the piano's throb. The crowd, dimly sensing the struggle, tried to share the urge. It became a thing of shoving, clapping hands, of patted feet, of hoarse shouts, of popping fingers, of knees and thighs that danced and bumped excited by their own heat and reeking sweat. Clothes would come off, hands would be furtively tucked between legs and buttocks would wink and be pinched.

Thurley's voice was drowned as he called to Brother. He followed the men through a maze of tables and chairs scattered in the rush towards the bandstand. When he reached him they were already seated, facing each other in one of the dim stalls that marked the corners of Harry's Place. He heard Eddie's sobs singularly clear and distinct within the swelling vortex of sound.

Brother saw him first, regarding Thurley from beneath his peaked cap first with a dumb animal incomprehension, then a mute indifference as his pink eyes returned to where his outstretched hand clasped Eddie's on the dark wood. Something sullenly fatal about the turning away of his eyes, something cold and limpid as allegory made Thurley hang on Brother's simplest gestures. He felt exquisitely nervous, attuned to a starkness of meaning that would only be revealed if he carefully attended to the dumb show enacted in this black corner. Eddie raised his face from the table; there was no glimmer of recognition, no sign of resentment, as if a total stranger could be no more foreign than himself to the unbridled grief and pain that ravaged through him. Thurley thought the face peering up at him almost smiled before it was lowered or at least an inexplicable adjustment of the features was caused by some fluid light source playing momentarily upon them. Thurley sat down on the outer edge of the bench on Brother's side facing Eddie. He sat stiffly, folding his hands, gazing at the scarred table top that had a second before seemed a calm, purple sea. He wanted so much to compose himself, to find that peace which would release him from himself, the peace that prevented him from being an intruder but would leave him responsive to the slightest nuance emanating from the two men.

Thurley felt completely inept. His night world had been a kind of game; there was no death beneath the frenzied life of its surface. He enjoyed the vicarious plunge, living on its fringes, feeling the excitement of the music but never dancing. But now the lie failed him because he had something to say to these men a few feet away from him. Indian Slick's insect body loomed up in his imagination. Out of nowhere, out of the poised shadow of violence, urgency and substance came. They *would* understand, and he would understand them. They would know why he had to speak, why he had to come, why the day and the week and the month and the year had to be forgotten so the moment could live. The men he joined in this corner were perhaps more naked and empty than he felt himself. It was not their world which swirled in blackness and heat around the booth. It was the same dark water that had floated Thurley for so long and from so far to the table where he sat this Easter night. They would understand. He could tell them. I come because . . . because . . . I must sit here because . . .

—We don't mind if he sits down, do we Brother? It might do the white man good to see a nigger cry. Eddie sat up, the sound of his voice, although barely audible, relieving him of a heavy load of silence his sobs had not eased. There was nothing pugnacious in his tone, in fact as he spoke the words seemed to belie any kind of construction Thurley could put on them. It was the sound of a man talking in his sleep, of a voice rising from a dream, disconnected from the reality in which another hears it, evocative of some impenetrable state of mind the hearer can only imagine.

—Don't you remember Bobbie? Brother's voice was unreal. He looked up from Eddie, trying to reach the other man.

—Eddie's had a loss. His mother passed today, his first day home in a year. He came all the way here to see her, and now she's had some accident, and she's dead. Brother spoke solemnly, in unhurried deliberate phrases, never turning to Thurley but keeping his eyes on Eddie, trying to make certain that his statement reached through Eddie's silence. Brother's eyes gave everything away. It was clear that he wanted Eddie to believe what was said to Thurley and didn't know how except to hurry on to another question before Eddie could speak. Remember how knocked out I was that night? Bobbie helped you to get me home.

—Yes, he helped.

—And you fussing all the time, Eddie. I ain't got the best manners, but sometimes you shame me. But Bobbie understood. He's all right. I mean if it was just anybody, I'd have chased him away then or now. Just anybody don't have no right inviting themselves to a place they ain't invited especially when men is talking serious, and they got good reason to be serious.

—I remember screaming at you. I remember telling you I hated you. And I did. If I had believed no harm would have come to me, I would have happily killed you.

—And now?

—Now I don't care. Brother's right, he's always been right. There's nothing for it, nothing at all. Get out of here, mister.

—Brother. Thurley blurted out the name like an echo. I must tell you something. The piano player, the one they call Indian Slick. For some reason he told me to tell you . . . certain people don't want to see you two together . . . here . . .

—Not with Eddie! Why that conkeline headed, axle-grease-wearing monkey. It don't concern him a damn who I'm with or why I'm with 'em. Me stay away from Eddie! Just cause Eddie tried to do something for hisself these niggers is afraid of him. Talking when Eddie was away about how Eddie ain't to be trusted, that he'd be working for the Man when he got back. It's that Slick who talks the most. He never did like Eddie. And he don't like me cause I told him to stay away from Alice. I'll do some talking to that chump. Knock his Slick head clean off. Brother rose in his chair as he spoke, shouting almost and drawing deep flushes into his cheeks beneath his ghostly lurid flesh. I'll kill that little junkie.

—Sit down, Bruv, sit down. These rats are bound to be suspicious of me. Just be cool and it'll blow over. You have to get what we need so don't go mouthing off. Be patient man, they'll see I'm still O.K. soon enough. I can't afford to mess up here; it's all I have. After a year I guess I still smell a bit of the Man. He wrinkled his nose, sniffing disdainfully at his wrist, his eyes coldly meeting Thurley across the table. Behind them the noise had diminished. Slick was coming off the stand and the crowd filtered slowly away into arguments about deserted tables and drinks. No one approached their corner, but Thurley felt the space they occupied palpably cramped by unseen phantoms stealthily materializing around them. Within this tightening space, he also felt more alone than at any moment since he had joined the two men. Brother still scowled, visibly at odds with himself, remaining seated when what he wanted most to do was search out his enemy. Eddie had withdrawn into a shell of silent contemplation. That he concentrated severely was obvious to Thurley watching his long fingers pick at the rough edge of the table and the vein he vividly remembered define itself in his high brow. The ease Thurley had felt, what he could almost call an air of familiarity with this man's intensity had vanished. It was as if Eddie's momentary weakness had drawn them together, his grief opening a passage through the calloused husk of his being. An adept at all species of pain Thurley had entered with a surgeon's skill and tact, but now the wound shut of its own accord and Thurley was neither in nor out.

Eddie finally spoke. —Thanks for passing on what you did. Did he say anything else?

—Not really.

—I wonder why he spoke to you. Why he thought you'd involve yourself, even care.

—Cause Bobbie's my friend, and Slick knew I'd bust 'em in his mouth if he started talking that sort of shit to me hisself.

—And you think this man is really your friend, Brother? What

161

kind of friend is he? What does he give to you, what does he take?

—Aw man, now I can't answer that. I don't hardly know what you mean. It ain't like going to a grocery store. Ain't no tags on everything.

—Then you think he gives a damn whether you live or die?

—Yeah, I believe that.

—It's more than I can believe. I killed her, that's all I can believe . . . I killed her.

—Man, man! You killed nobody, you don't even know she's dead do you?

—She's dead. I caused it. My words, my wish brought her down those stairs. I couldn't even look at her. I was afraid of her eyes . . . afraid they would still be open, burning, accusing me . . . she couldn't even speak . . . with her last breath she . . . Eddie couldn't finish, his head fell into his hands, and when he spoke again his voice had an almost hysterical edge.

—Do you know what I just did, what happened when I took my head in my hands? I started to pray. Like a little boy. Like some snotty little kid I started whimpering, *now I lay me down.* Thurley watched the distended pupils grow dim, Eddie's whole body relax as the tightness drained from his shoulders, and Eddie shifted his weight forward to rest both shirt sleeved arms on the table's surface. He leaned closer to them, the eggshell fragility of his high brow bright and frightening. Now I lay me down to sleep. Every night I had to say my prayers, Mama came in and stood beside me to hear. For a long time I didn't understand it at all. Then I began to realize I was asking for things. They told me I was down on my knees speaking to a great and powerful God who had everything in his hands and who could give me anything I asked. So instead of staying in bed when Mama left, I would climb out and ask for something besides sleep and blessings. I kept myself busy all day thinking about what I'd like. Each night I couldn't wait to be finished with the first prayers so I could get down to business. I don't remember how long I believed, but I remember the day I started hating Mama over me while I crouched down to speak to a God who never gave what I asked for. I never quite forgave him, even when I went to church, I didn't forgive. As soon as Mama stopped coming in at night, I stopped praying. But tonight the words came . . . like tears . . . came back. Alice's, mine . . . I can't help them. Do you know the words? *Now I lay me down to sleep, I pray the Lord my soul to keep, and if I die before I wake, I pray the Lord my soul to take.* Then you begin blessing people—one by one—mother, father, sisters, brothers, everybody in the whole world, or special ones, those sick or in need, even animals and things you can bless. I blessed you Brother, almost every night if we weren't fighting I stuck you on the end of my prayers. But they stopped one day. Haven't crossed my lips till now. Maybe it's because I want to speak to Mama, I want her to be beside me in the darkness. When I did feel a sort of comfort, it was her being there and not the words. She always went to Eugene first. And even when we got too old for her to be there, he kept on praying. He's dead you know, died fighting for God Bless America in some stinking jungle on some stinking island doing some stinking job some stinking white man wouldn't do himself. Thurley is your name, isn't it? I don't blame anybody, believe me, Thurley. Lots of people died on Guam. Black, yellow, and probably white most of all. It's the way Gene died that gets me. Being black he had to be a flunky, here, there, anywhere the white man is. So what's it mean—it means he died a flunky. But that's a while ago, isn't it? He's bones now or dust. He died and didn't change anything, and I will do the same and Brother will, even you will. If my head ever goes down again, those words won't come. They came from a long time ago. I had to say them one last time loud and clear so I could be sure they were gone for good . . . make sure I wouldn't get caught alone with them again some night. All that has to be said now is Amen. Say it for me, Bruv. Don't be ashamed. Amen, Brother,

Amen. Say it, man, you must say it. It's finished, don't you
see . . . finished, nothing, nothing more . . . Amen . . .

—Amen, Eddie. I said it, listen to me, Eddie, Amen, Amen.
Bobbie, c'mon, you say it too. Eddie needs to hear it. Amen.
C'mon, Bob. Amen.

It was there, in the urgency of Eddie's cry, in Brother's excited, pleading voice. Thurley heard himself shout *Amen*. Heard
the strange sound from his lips grow natural as it blended
with Brother's repetition of the same word. Eddie began to
laugh, a laugh that made Thurley shudder, then laugh himself,
as its bright knife edge softened to diffuse a steady, beneficent
glow over Eddie's face. It was finally a rich, throat deep laugh
reaching above the discordant sounds of Harry's, a laugh whose
power only Eddie knew as it ranged through the immense
silences within his breast.

—I said Amen for Saunders once, Bruv. You remember him,
don't you? Felt sorry for the poor bastard, he just couldn't take
it. A week in the streets and he was hooked again. Just couldn't
do with it, or without it. When he returned so soon after
seeming so well, it scared me. I decided then to stick it out a
whole year, not to kid myself. To get stronger than I thought
I'd ever have to be. And would you believe it, this is my first
day home, night one and I'm ready. No more strength left. I'm
down on my knees waiting. What kind of a man am I? Do you
know, white man? You seem to be educated; you're white. But
then again you're here too, just about as low as a white man can
get, calling yourself a friend of Brother's and drinking Harry's
bad whiskey from his dirty glasses, sitting here talking to me, a
man even these niggers don't want around them.

—In some ways I believe I can understand. It's an awful thing
to lose a mother. I can understand how you feel. A look of
panic crossed Brother's face. A look his ugliness made ludicrous.
The pasty faced clown, grimacing absurdly, pursued by his
shadow.

164

—Do you really think you understand? Eddie tensed, his face suddenly closer, a flash of heat and light across the table.

—I lost a mother.

—But did you . . . Eddie paused, two words jarred in his mind struck up by the same impulse, words that at first seemed contradictory, then rushed inextricably down onto his tongue so they felt like different ways of asking the same question, and when he used one of the pair, *love,* instead of *kill* her, it contained the meaning of both. Did you love her?

—If I say I did, there are certain things I can't explain, but if I say I didn't, there are more.

—What kinds of things? The question came from a shadow Eddie, a source alien and unexpected whose life Eddie could only observe, blood pouring from a razor slash he could not feel, aware of curiosity not pain as Thurley spoke.

—Her brooch. A gold, green jewelled brooch. Something she felt closer to than any other. She gave it to me when she had become very old and near to death. I kept it in the box that had always belonged to it. A velvet lined box, built up so it had a sort of pillow inside on which the brooch rested. When you closed the box, even though it was very old, a hinge made it snap shut the last inch or so by itself. A soft, muffled snap as the velvet edges came together. I gave it to a little boy a few days ago . . . a year ago . . . I don't know, to someone I never saw before, or will see again and who will probably lose it or sell it if he hasn't already. In a way it was all I had left of her.

—Then she didn't die till you were a man. The question registered in Eddie's ears. The sound of a voice reaching out to meet the other still strangely his own and not his own.

—No, not till I had brought home a blushing bride and Mother had danced at our wedding. Thurley stopped himself on the verge of a gossiping monologue. Something urged him to begin at the beginning, rehearse his one great love affair from the first fearful descent into her body to the culmination of their

marriage when Eleanor, laughing hysterically, called him into
the bathroom to see the miscarried remnants of his *son* before
she flushed *him* down the toilet. It all seemed vaguely relevant,
something he ought to share with the voice.

—Where is your wife?

—She's gone. I haven't seen or heard of her for longer than I
can remember. She may be in a home somewhere.

—And you don't care, do you? Like that piece of jewelry, she's
just gone. Come to Harry's and get drunk, anything you've ever
lost can be bought cheaper. A wife . . . a gold pin, Harry
has it all. Even God, God's here. That's church music you know,
sanctified music, only here you can dance and drink to it. Forget
'em, white man, that's why you're here, and me, and all these
fools. Amen, Brother. Tell this white man about bags. Tell him
how Harry draws them closed so it's dark and what you breathe
is at least your own foul breath. Everybody, everything gone,
closed up tight. That's what Harry does. Makes it so everything's
gone . . .

—People don't go like that. You can just kill yourself, always
part of yourself, not them, they're not what goes. Even if we
have to act as if it is, if we have to pretend, have to shut out
certain things sometimes to get to the next stage. Love, hate,
pity, if there's no one to whom we can tie these feelings they
grow too large, too powerful, become something that destroys.
What we feel inside must have a release, even if it's one that
once was or might have been. That's why we can't afford to
ever let go. Even the pieces of other people we've helped break
apart. The spirit can't live on air, and especially the air that's
inside our bodies. It flourishes when it touches other things—
people, work. Thurley began to grow uneasy. He knew he meant
what he said, but why now, why to these men? He knew he was
generating a rarefied, distilled air, the atmosphere where he
liked to believe the still untainted parts of his mind and spirit
moved freely. But to bring it out into the open, to hear the high
thoughts and exalted feelings transformed into words was like

unravelling an infinite tape measure to take the five feet ten inches of his dying flesh. Of course, he thought, it's not wrong to express how I'd like to be, to show that I have an idea what a better kind of life should be, that I think I know the kind of strength I need to live it. No, I can't forget dead things, or things that were never alive. I move among them, like a mole in the darkness, beneath the earth. It is their substance I must burrow through to see the light, to give the spirit somewhere to breathe. I cannot be ashamed, I cannot hold back my little simply because it's little.

—Your mouth's full of words. You say you think you understand. The spirit needs this, needs that. Here's something for you to think about. Some people, the black ones you see around you, they live without spirit. There's just shit and Harry's, Harry's or shit. I despise what you are and they do too. Things about you make me almost sick, but I have to sit here speaking to you, have to listen to you or any other white man who thinks he knows because I can't claim anything better. Because I'm Eddie Lawson—nothing. I've tried the shit today, died for a year so I could have it rubbed in my face again. And Harry's has been here all the time. Harry's waiting for me. That's the funny part. Harry's always waiting.

Thurley felt the words enter, a gust of burning needles, striking, swirling about. His speech had fallen flat. The classroom rhetoric he dredged up could not live in the dark corner. He could not speak again; he wasn't afraid of Eddie's words, only the inevitable silence he knew must follow. Thurley stared into the other man's face, watching the eyes, the blood, the tremors of the skin subside. He had only the vaguest idea of Eddie's character, only Brother's garbled anecdotes and the words passed in two short confrontations. But he also knew nothing would ever be able to separate him from the young man's pain. He must help Eddie. Must get him out. And to where? Of course not any particular place, no place at least through which Thurley discontentedly had passed. No, just free from this choking air, free from the hungers that fed on him. There is the night, the black, all blackening night. We can breathe there, we can lead there and be led unashamedly.

Someone dropped a coin in the jukebox; a woman began to sing, her rasping, heavy voice belting out a current popular ballad. After an initial burst of pleased exclamations, rustling of dresses, chairs scraping, glasses set down, feet shuffling towards the dance floor, Harry's grew quiet. Couples glided, pressed tightly together on the dance floor as everyone seemed moved by the melancholy ballad of lost love and tears.

Thurley listened intently, partly to catch the lyrics and partly to escape the terrible vertigo as he lost contact with Eddie. The voice made Thurley think of Bessie Smith, but it was far from that standard—maudlin phrases that struck him as cliché rather than true, and a voice mechanically amplified through too many echo chambers to retain the suffering edge Bessie always brought out in the blues, that poignant friability always threatening to destroy the singer and the song, the susceptibility to pain that made them one, that made the blues like crying.

The memory of how good it could be made Thurley weak. When he spoke, his voice wavered. —What you said a minute ago, Eddie. About despising me.

—Forget it, it doesn't matter. I'm sick of me, that's what I'm sick of. What I've been, what I am, and the only things I can be. Just leave me and Brother now would you please. There's nothing else to say or do. Just this goddamn night and a morning I don't want to see.

—Amen.

—Forget it.

—Amen, Eddie. Amen. I say that because . . . because there's something left. Even if it's something you don't like, it's there. Say Amen to that.

—You know nothing.

—I know it's been bad. Today and for so long today seems always. And I'm not talking about you, about your pain. I'm

168

saying that it's been bad for me. I don't know what's smacked you down, but . . . I've been down . . . it's true . . . I've been down. But you've got me pegged don't you. A worn out fairy, mouth full of words, rotting on one of Harry's stools. Maybe that's not exactly what you think, maybe you don't even feel I'm worth pegging. No matter what you think, or anybody thinks, there's this . . . this I have to say. The worst is true. Has been and probably will be tomorrow. But tonight I'm more. The music's for me tonight. My music. I'm not afraid. One moment, one morning, one slice of light even if I don't see it, even if it's not for me. No spirit, Eddie, and all these people no spirit. It wouldn't hurt the way it does if there wasn't. You can deny it, you can cut everything off with one of Slick's cures. But you know you'd be killing something that fights back. That wants to live. I don't know what's happened today, or all the yesterdays, but it hasn't been enough to put you out. You're still soft, still squirming beneath the pain and fear. Get through tonight, Eddie. I have a car, I'll take you to your home, or to my place, anywhere you want to go. Just get through tonight and tomorrow . . .

—And tomorrow I'll have the smell of your white hands over my body.

—No, no you must come. I know in some ways you can't trust me yet, believe me even partially, and maybe you never will. Maybe I'll spoil it. But come out of here, I know I'm right in that at least.

He looked at Thurley. It was hard to pick his words out of the deafening roar the jukebox now produced. At first it was only the tone of Thurley's plea that struck Eddie as familiar, then the mad rush of the day's events inundated his imagination with a flood of images and phrases. His own words came back to him. Then Thurley beckoned more clearly than ever across the dark table. He saw Thurley too, swaying and tottering, moments, inches from the abyss. Eddie moved instinctively, grief wide in his eyes, the way he moved towards the mystery

169

of Grierson, the way he moved towards Alice, towards his mother, towards Bette, towards Saunders, the way he always moved with Brother. He couldn't edge very far out of the booth before his arm became taut in the grasp of Brother's who still remained motionless.

–Where you going? Why you running, Eddie. Slick sells the only thing for it right here. There ain't nowhere to go man. You know there ain't nothing out there.

Eddie looked down at his hand crossed by Brother's livid flesh on the dark table. –Let me go Bruv. It's best I go. I don't want to get you in trouble . . . I have to walk out of here by myself. The night, Brother . . . we were afraid of it so long, then it got to be our time. Nothing out there . . . Are they gone, Brother, like the prayers each night, where are they, Brother—Mama, Alice, Bette, and us, where are we . . . Brother stared blankly at his friend, his mind turning . . .

Eddie told me his mother dead then not dead some story about killing her then how she fell and killed herself how he had to have some stuff he said he was dying and had to get to Harry's to find some said he wanted to kill himself crazy he was and said nothing could help but what Slick sells crying almost he said nothing else would help but now I'll be damned if I know talking to this faggot professor and saying crazy things I guess he just must be stark raving.

He watched as Eddie disappeared through the door then felt the weight of a hand on his shoulder as Thurley rose and motioned that they follow. Pulling his cap down tighter on his head, Brother fell in behind the professor almost laughing at the white man's graceless movements as he wove clumsily, bumping and apologizing, among scattered tables towards the door.

He don't look back and we don't try to catch him and he don't try to run away I was scared back there he would get mad and hit Bobbie or say something worse and cause trouble after what Slick said and them niggers don't play games if Eddie hit somebody that's all they'd need to jump him no telling how bad it would be I'd help but then so many of 'em and in that place everybody crazy so I was so glad Eddie just sat and said nasty things at Bobbie and listened and came out here in the night without no trouble though I never seen Eddie so low he went out the door like there weren't no more doors ever for him to go in but it's hard losing a mother is what I hear and I can understand even though I forget and Mrs. Lawson sometimes it seemed better not for her to be the way she treated Bette and Eddie home after a year he was down South where they hang niggers and so bad I hear you gotta cross the street if a white woman's coming funny cause here you see it happen so much nigger with a gray broad and ain't hardly nothing to it see 'em in cars or in some club hanging on each other and Bobbie walking here beside me from down there but walking beside me and even seeking niggers it seems or why else come to Harry's and a nigger like me almost living in his house ain't that a bitch him following Eddie beside me like he don't care what street this is and where we're going deeper where there ain't nothing but black and he keeps walking his eyes stuck to Eddie's back up ahead who don't run or look behind.

—Where is he going, Brother?

Like I might know where Eddie wants to go after all this happening all's I can tell is far from home Dumferline Street in the other direction and soon the tracks we can see and the bridge but first some dark stores and the sanctified church where it's good to listen all day cause they sit there all Sunday and sing their asses off and make noise and sometimes it's louder than Harry's and smells almost as bad Eddie wandering this way I wonder if he remembers Tiny and his DaddyGene and that crazy talk but it's dark now Eddie peeking inside there ain't nothing there to see he should know but like he's looking for someone and what's he got off the pavement something white in his hand looks like bread he's tearing and dropping pieces behind like he's feeding birds or he don't want me and Bobbie to get lost giving us something to follow wherever he's going, he's going . . .

—I don't know, he just seems to be walking and maybe we should leave him be.

—You know we can't; we have to get him through this night, Brother.

And what changes tomorrow like the sun's gonna bring something different if there is a sun tomorrow or if it rains down the gutter some will go but don't change nothing me one day too I wonder how long you drain before you get somewhere it must be the deepest hole anywhere you can fall into or be guttered and blacker than Henry Bow's neck I still hate Slick what he said about Alice just cause she wouldn't and he thinks a chick should be glad he asks but she told him where to take it my sister ain't no whore Alice should be Eddie's girl but there's some things she thinks she knows but don't Eddie loves her I know but Alice is so damned scared that's why she fights like she does so somebody will fight with her so she can be mad and not scared and someday she'll understand and Eddie should be with her now she been so scared since he's gone why I just don't understand why they don't stay together cause there ain't nothing in this world bag ask Brother if you don't believe it nothing to this world bag I know so well cause I been out here and couldn't care less now that I know so I'll just follow Eddie if Bobbie thinks it's best and probably he's right though he don't know where Eddie's going and I don't and Eddie probably neither but he can't look back just walking slow like nowhere particular and no hurry like he wants never to stop but to keep moving in those long slow steps he takes the shadows eat him it seems sometimes a bite of Eddie they take as he moves in and out the black shadows Eddie got a big head like a big egg and it looks so heavy sometimes cause the rest of him is skinny it sitting there so big sometimes it scares me like so heavy it's gonna tip over and fall my head looks bigger than it is but I don't know the last time my hat off only in front of Eddie I remember unless somebody takes it or knocks it but this morning I almost forgot Mrs. Lawson made me and if it hadn't been Eddie's Mama kiss my ass I would have said if it hadn't been Bette's Mama and Bette there too who knows how I am about my cap Mrs. Lawson too knows damn well but sometimes I think she got nothing better to do than hurt me standing there like I owe her something waiting for some words to come to say I'm sorry and after all it was her that did the hurting ain't my fault I got a bald, ugly head she knew better than to say it and make me do it.

—Is he going towards his home?

—Other way where he lives. Nothing down here soon but a dump and the tracks and don't go no further than the ball field after that. Just tracks after that.

—Do you think we should call him?

—He knows we're here. Ain't nobody but fools walk these streets this time of night. Fools and them that lives in the Forest.

—What?

—Bums' Forest—behind those two big billboards under the bridge. Little path through them big signs then trees and grass till the ball field.

—A hobo camp?

—Call it what you like, it's the Bums' Forest . . . I don't like it specially at night and the winos that live there hard up for coins where is Eddie going up between them signs don't he know how them fools are he's liable to get his throat cut.

—Nobody will bother the three of us together. C'mon Brother, we'll catch him now.

Eddie ain't no kid to be running after but this white man thinks he gotta do something though I know there ain't nothing to be done but climb in that one bag Eddie tried to fight but back in this hell it don't matter a year or hundred years ain't long enough and no fight is hard enough cause the bag is strongest and best just to stop fighting till there ain't no more air I'll follow Eddie in here cause I could care less if somebody wants my throat I should say thank you cause it don't do me a bit of good just carry around my bald head and this white man Thurley playing some crazy game about getting Eddie through this night as if tomorrow will be different as if the sun would be a new one that's gonna change something don't he know he's supposed to be educated that chasing Eddie in this black jungle is damn foolishness that even if Eddie lets us catch 'em he don't care if we do cause he ain't running but just going somewhere to hide from the bag the only thing for Eddie is what's good always what Slick sells and keeps the sun off your back I hope Eddie ain't too bad and me and this white man make it worse cause losing a mother is bad and Eddie even thinks it was his fault though he don't really know saying different things and crying like a baby big tears like when he fought Henry I remember or when DaddyGene died I never could understand Eddie crying till he was sick me and Gene cried too but not so much he had to be put to bed funny about Eddie's bags they really cover him and I wonder sometimes where Eddie is like he's gone and I can't find him he's covered and nothing shows not even as much as him still slow walking in these weeds I hear the crickets I wonder how they get so loud if they have big mouths or just lots of them cause I don't believe Eddie knows what he was talking about when he said their legs rubbing make all that noise my legs make no noise through the weeds just wind blowing the trees and crickets doing what they do I guess they gotta holler too I guess they fight and cuss and sing and dance just like everybody me and Eddie did when it was our time but not so much cause I was so ugly and Eddie didn't really seem to care just Alice I always thought he's scared of other girls didn't even know what they were I think him passing up good pussy when Emma Jeanne in the garage and everybody me last climbed on that fat stuff Eddie didn't even know what it was or he woulda' been right there with everybody but I know he did it to my sister to Alice and I always thought I'd be mad when I knew somebody climbed on her but funny Eddie was all right and in a way I didn't even think about it like I knew it would happen someday and we knew it was supposed to be just waiting Alice me and Eddie where is he now these damn weeds up to my knees and getting higher damn bugs I can feel how hungry they are waiting here liable to cut my foot off on this glass everywhere my shoes ain't so good just gumsoles and not even much of that I wonder where Eddie is going and why this white man following damn I'm hungry and cold ain't had nothing dammit I'd like a Hershey bar.

—I don't see him, Brother. Can you see him through the trees, he must have turned off the path. Here . . . he must have turned off here.

Dammit a spider web that must have been where the hell is Eddie going hide and seek now I'm getting tired and it won't be the first time I slept on the grass and here is as good as any-place I suppose cause I'm tired and any fool can see I ain't got nothing to rob nothing but these rags on my back and these shoes barely keeping out the glass there is Eddie on a big stone and what the hell now look at that white man just standing staring at Eddie well we caught him and here we are in the middle of nowhere on rocks round a dead fire some bums used to keep off the cold both of 'em not saying a word just sitting there and it's getting chilly now the fools are shivering sometimes I think it's me that's the smartest the only one thinks of trying to light a fire on these ashes where is something that will burn quickly a newspaper is what I need to catch these twigs and them just sitting like they's expecting company to come out of this black night dammit they should be looking for kindling but this is enough to start crackle you little bastards get something going to keep Brother warm looks like we'll be here a while with them just sitting looking at the night ain't even a star to be seen like a black roof that's all it is and not too far away up through the trees I wonder how high or if anybody could

175

touch it maybe Bobbie knows he should know something
teacher he is it seems him always showing me what he don't
know how silly he can be and needs a fool like me sometimes
to tell him things or show him it seems like he should know if
it's too high to touch or if anybody has tried he should know or
maybe Eddie sometimes Eddie knows what you wouldn't think
he knows like what he said about crickets and I wonder how
he got to know such things as I never heard of and Eddie ain't
so dumb though not like my sister Alice who thinks she knows
so much and does know a lot but she should listen to Eddie
and not be afraid to hear the things Eddie knows some of them
so strange I wonder how he found out he says in books and I
believe it cause books is news to me I couldn't care less but I
know when I'm cold and when I need a fire even if I can't
get chocolate and there they sit on those stones neither of them
would have moved just froze to death waiting.

—Thank you Brother, it feels good.

Damn right it does and Eddie knows it too though he don't
say nothing I can see he's stopped shaking and moved a little
closer his face I can see now in the flames big head and the
bones show black and white his face is in the fire everything
dark and deep sunken or shining like his forehead and his eyes
are just sparks little lights I can tell when they move he looks
at Bobbie but away quick like he don't believe a white man's
sitting here on a rock the three of us like bums toasting round
my fire that needs more wood Bobbie kicks a piece toward me
no good it would put out the damn fire but he's trying just little
pieces what I need I don't want to burn the damn Forest down
or attract no attention these bums like flies think cause we got
a fire we got other things and looking for a handout or a drink
I wish I had something myself not that rotgut but what Slick
sells then I wouldn't give a damn about bugs about them
crickets bout bums bout nothing just sit here long as they want
to till tomorrow or the next day even if it takes that long if
Bobbie thinks a night or day will change something and Eddie's

willing to sit I'll stay right with them but it would be so much better with what Slick sells I hope they ain't too mad at Eddie Eddie got it bad Eddie tried to fight his bag and it scares them cause they live off other people's bags and Eddie fights silly fights I told 'em and ones he knows he can't win but Eddie fights and it just gets harder Henry hits harder and it's better to take low and not to make it worse by trying to land a lucky punch his Mama is hard and Alice who's scared and now this white man wants something from Eddie don't he know Eddie don't go that way that Eddie ain't like me I take what comes but Eddie fights and ain't got nothing for Bobbie no not for all the money Bobbie makes Eddie ain't gonna stop being a man not like me Eddie thinks it makes a difference not like me if that's what the white man wants he's wasting his time but that ain't it I got a feeling he wants more wants Eddie to get through this night to wait for the sun to come like it's gonna make a difference . . .

Thurley gazes into the fire: perhaps I will die tonight. Perhaps I am already dead. This is the way it ends the way it begins always will be like this. Men ranged round a fire, the darkness heavy, silence. Perhaps death is on a rock for eternity watching the flames decay other faces. It broods, it chews, it melts, destroying. Perhaps I am dead in this wood. And these devils. Silent devils that mock and change in the fire. How easily they come. The living and dead come to me, throng this wood, this dark wood. They should be wearing robes, or wrapped in flame, something to explain how they move so easily, how they came here. To save him. To save me. What are they doing . . . I ask . . . shapes, colors, old rooms, doors I have entered, beds where . . . she comes . . . but she will not speak, will not look at me, the eyes gone, all features gone, a haze where they should be, but I know it is Eleanor, the hair, the shoulders, the deep pinch of her waist. Perhaps dead. I do not know. Cannot. This boy I must save. Dark boy whose face changes. His eyes

. . . those for a year I remembered. And tonight how he moved through the crowd, through the street and losing sight of him in these woods. I shook, I trembled for fear he was gone. An old man. Perhaps a dead man. And to be dead the need is no less urgent. If I am dead, I still desire. Desire their shapes, their colors. Eleanor whose body I came to fear. What did I fear? Losing him in these woods. Though an old man I still need, still want. Save him. Cling. They glide so effortless through the flame. Does someone have something to say. Each one giving way, waiting for the other to speak. The boy whose dirty hand, who I believed I loved. He gives way, will not speak, defers to the next and all of them defer, all give way, wait for the next shape to speak. How many? How they swarm. How they crowd me. Loved on my knees. All of them bowed to, pleaded with all, but their bodies disappear, they fill me, then they pass, not speaking, deferring to the next to the next. So many, filling up, the dark woods full.

Their thoughts twist in the darkness:
The fire, the fire
I've made many mistakes
Burning . . .
I am sick
Turn to the sound of crickets in the grass
Death is so close my flesh angers the bones.
The fire
But I will sit on this hard stone
Brother stirs it. It licks the darkness. The pup dances
I . . .
On her steel brace.
Am dying.
An old woman, my mother who will never taste again or hear night sounds.
The embers, ashes, dust, a rag . . .
If I could turn again . . . the flame feeds . . . something

must be ending, always ending if the flame climbs, if it eats and cracks.

Upon a stick.

I must turn again. There is Bette. All dead. She watched them all die. How many can the eyes bear? Do the eyes scar . . . will she . . .

Quotation as close . . .

Will she be free . . .

Hattie lifted me. Her eyes were cow eyes, her black hands like new underwear on my body. Where will it take me? I cannot ask.

A chocolate bar

Why such heavy ones, why does he lift

Hattie's breast is round and soft like a pillow. Once I watched it squirm its way free. I did not know what to expect. Then it finally came, finally showed itself black and blacker tipped after flirting so long beneath the buttonless cotton blouse. Touch . . . gone . . . the pain.

Turn again . . .

The fire.

Damn . . . just little sticks.

The Brobdingnags. So big, so close. The smell, the pits in the skin. Gulliver's little box.

Part of myself.

Do I dare . . . on rocks in a circle. Brother tends it. He brought it from the gods at the risk of . . .

Why should Bette have to see it all? Why happen and scar her eyes? Scabs do form, do hide and make ugly. My sister will have to unwrap, turn back the folds, lift the head.

Old.

Like a little girl's hair, Mama's will fall long and straight like a little girl's.

Promised myself a kind of peace. The world hid nothing. I should have been grateful. The worst things . . . could and did happen. I am witness and victim. Truth is only the evidence I have suffered. There can be no more. A kind of peace afterall to step down, to know it has happened, to have admitted the worst. But the others, there are others . . . It begins again . . . always another victim . . .

What were the games we played . . . me and my Alice

Another witness

I remember only songs, only movements, something . . .

Another truth.

Paddy cake Paddy cake Baker's man bake them cakes as fast as you can, Roll them bake them one two three, Put 'em in the oven for Alice and me

Cold

If only till the morning, if Eddie will only stay, if he can stand up in the light and look back on this . . . over it all, through it in the light.

I remember how funny it was. Just nothing, just wrinkles and nothing. Like the back in a way only a small one. Just slits. Ugly Alice held her skirt up high so I could see. I got closer and closer. I looked. She squeezed it, spread it open. I looked deeper. I moved around and she turned. She did anything I asked. Nothing. She said a word I didn't understand. Closer. She bent and I tried to see deeper. Nothing. She said touch. Touch. I said no. Just look. Just see. Nothing.

Rocks, for an eternity on rocks. Alone waiting for morning.

Sometimes I wished it hadn't grown. Hair, coarse, dry and sharp sometimes when I entered. I missed its bareness, bare so I could see. But I couldn't ask, and she wouldn't if I asked, how could I ask . . . begin again.

Looking down at a bird. From a mountainside down on a white bird fluttering over a lake. It was a poem. How I saw it was a poem I couldn't write. That is how you tell how high. When there are birds beneath, gliding white over the dazzling water. How it is serene, unwavering and you see it all in the sudden parting of a cloud. But it is not towards it you can move. Never towards it. The mountain was near the sea. The bird a gull. Streams, froth white, unmoving it seemed far off on the sides of other mountains. Frozen it seemed, veins of ice, but could hear their roar. Could hear thin echo of the sea funnelled up between the steep, rock walls.

My Alice

The summit still in a cloud.

The fire

The loud waters

Love. Love was all silence. Once it meant that for Alice and me. Stillness and silence. There can be a sound, there can be the glider's wheezing, Mama's voice in the darkness when Gene and I knelt, some sounds even begin the silence. Silence is a door.

The fire like pebbles on tin.

Through it are the things you can't say. The things words scare away.

Rocks

I love you Alice. I always whispered, afraid to break the silence. Alice fights. She fights the silence with words. Words like stones.

Morning will come.

What Slick sells

Silence on these rocks and only the fire speaking. Brother. The white man. Why? Where does his white man's mind go at night in this black night in this hole. Afraid. He would cry if the fire went out. Afraid of the dark. Him shaking, fearing black hands from the weeds to carry him away. Leave him. Kick out the fire and leave him.

The fire . . .

Bury it, grind the flame into the earth. We will leave him crying in the darkness. Afraid of the black bogey man. Slick sells.

The clouds part and you understand. The next stage . . .

The white man must have money. Something. If he gives it to us we will not harm.

Lifted, her cow eyes shining. Hands like . . .

His friend . . . Brother believes that the white man is his friend.

Fireflies over the lawn, over the deep cool spaces.

With these hands take . . . what can they take . . . my sister's pain?

Luminous in the corner . . .

Brother will help me if I begin, not hurt the fairy, just take the money. Get what Slick sells. Crush out the fire.

Snow

Please give . . . we won't hurt you if you give and be silent

The voice, the cool hand taking mine. It is a soft crunch beneath our feet. Trackless, pure, closing behind us as we walk. Snow stretches . . . brilliant, snow stretches in some cold brilliant valley. Only his voice, gentle and the snow yielding as we move.

I do not want to hurt. Never again with these hands. Alice beneath me. Almost death. Mine, hers. Mama. Not her. Some heap of rags crumpled at the foot of the stairs. Paddy cake, paddy cake. Bette will lift, like a little girl's . . . falling.

His cool hand

Turn again.

Like color to a leaf whispering, come, come it is time, time to . . .

If only I had stayed. Or never gone. Slick sells. It would have been my pain. I wouldn't have hurt. Wouldn't have killed Mama. My pain neither ending nor beginning, hungry for no life, its red jaws fed with what is mine to give, mine to hurt.

He must see the morning, the light . . . my hand . . . purified through the fire. . . could it touch . . . could it lead through the valley?

Both go. Brother must go with the white man. Me alone.

182

The fire mine. Its red flame . . . I will feed. Something, nothing the fire lives.

It burns, darkness submits, the darkness abides the cancer of the flame. It feels no pain, the darkness cannot wince, cannot suffer. Night will not lie charred and unrecognized at dawn. It only will have moved, creeping across the brittle earth, its belly unfeeling, enveloping, swallowing all. No pain, no feeling. Unfaltering it will crawl across broken glass, across the razor edge of human cries; the flame does not consume. It does not penetrate the night. It consumes itself or the broken sticks it can drag into its arc. Night is there in the fire, in the core of its blaze, untouched. Night is in the glare it throws across their faces, in the flickering purple horror of the masks it imprints.

Chocolate

Must go away from here. Stop only once to get what Slick sells. Night, night, night.

It cannot be changed. We can only endure till night drags itself away.

No difference. No sun on my back, no night. No on again, off again, again, again days and nights . . . no nights, no days . . . the memories they bring . . . the ghost each hour possesses.

Wait, Eddie's face in the fire. The mask melting, dying, so afraid. Do not go.

Every minute someone rises to accuse. To ask me once again to remember. To hurt them again.

Wait for the cool hand. He will come Eddie. The fire . . . listen to the fire.

Mama.

Could it be . . . through the fire . . . pure again . . . ever pure . . . am I still lying to myself . . . can I know . . . lie, truth, pure . . . only night and day . . . the bird, the lake, a cloud that opens and we know where we are, the summit still wreathed, another cloud, the mask on Eddie's face, hiding, his hands moving as if they could hide in each other. What can I say? Can I tell him anything that is not a lie? Can I say, yes, can I say more than night and day, that day will follow night? Can I say look at me, can I say look at your friend Brother, can I say the snow closes silently behind our footsteps, can I point down to the glistening water, can I fill his ears with the sound of clear rushing water, can I say look, can I say listen . . . listen . . . look . . . darkness and silence

Fire

All the days are one day. Mama will come, she will set down the hot cereal, she will wipe the discolored spoons on the tail of her apron. Bette will be in the high chair. I will turn from my stomach to stroke the soft mound. I will kiss her naked back, I will whisper Alice I love, I will tease Bette, Eugene will tease, Mama will yell, I will take it in my hands fill the bowl with it steaming and hot, I will smell, I will taste, it will all be one, coming in going out, my blue plastic bowl, Eugene's red one, Bette's green, the cold whiteness where I am at last alone, squatting, warmly pouring through myself, the shiny spoon Gene always gets, mine I do not look at till its grayness is coated with thick oatmeal. Bette squeals, it goes on the floor, she turns to me, her lips softest then, no other time so soft, and I loved the sleep still in her Alice eyes, soon, soon, soon every-morning Alice morning, soon soon soon, Daddy will be here, better spoons, and when the chain is pulled all will go away, not left there to be found floating and putrid like you find what the others leave, and they find yours, and locks on the doors, neither be walked in on or catch Mama there standing in the tub wet, shining and cannot look away and she doesn't move and Alice, Alice look, look closer, closer, deeper, not that, just look, all one, soon soon he will be home again, it will be better . . . all the mornings floating, putrid because it is broken, because we do not have money, and it cannot be fixed

Darkness and silence.

All the hours one hour. Bette crying. She will not stop. It

seems her breath will stop soon but crying still and Brother at the door calling. Ball game, ball game and Gene is best, Gene wins always, the hit, the catch, he does it and I wish I . . . there is no time. It is all here, I cannot begin, I cannot end. Bette screams, Brother calls. Mama will be waiting she will be angry because we are late and all the time I wanted to go back before dinner but Gene said wait Gene said finish the game and then she stands at the door she wants to hit and Gene says nothing he ducks in quick while she warms up he is under her arm and in the house and now I have to pass through the door where she stands glaring and does not move. All time, I cannot breathe without the air of all those days rushing down in my lungs, DaddyGene held me Alice held me Mama held me Saunders died.

But I must be heard, must be seen. I must say I am not afraid. These rocks, I cannot let him leave the fire.

Bette screams. She cannot lift. She tries but cannot lift. Too heavy, too heavy for Bette to lift. For me . . .

If he starts to get up, if he moves away from the fire into the darkness again I will grab . . . I will make him carry me through the night. If only I could say something . . . if words were only made to touch . . . if only for a moment I had the singer's voice, the beauty of her voice I believe I could make him understand.

A little girl . . . I must . . . lift . . . help her lift

It will come, it will follow, morning will . . . and the strength . . . witness . . . I have been through, climbed through the night, the darkness . . . I have been there and now . . . now I see

Bette tries, like a little girl's falling, she tries, she raises Mama in her arms.

Floating, a gull over the blue lake.

Bette whispers, I think she is whispering, but it is because she has no breath because she cannot say the word, because it is her mother who lies there.

The strength . . . the light radiant on his back . . . morning

Bette screams. All time. The stone's hard push into my backside, the fire crackling. Daddy's coming soon . . . soon he'll be here. No more time, no more waiting soon soon it pushes, it is hard to sit alone, to feed it, to watch it die, something . . . nothing . . . flame.

If Eddie moves I will cling; he will have to drag me. Hold on even to the edge . . .

They don't move. They cannot speak. The flame crackles. I don't move, don't speak. All time, near then far, near then far, near then far. The crickets stop. We are part of the fire. We are part of the silence. I cannot move. I cannot speak . . .

I wonder how far away it is somebody should know somebody should find out and tell people cause I'm sure they want to know look at them both closer to my fire now and both looking at the flames I wonder what it feels like to burn if it always hurts once your hand is in it deep and if it pops and sparks like wood and if the color is the same and if it hurts and where does it go if you keep it in smoke rises through the trees to the sky towards the black roof where the sun will come if the sun comes tomorrow does it hurt or smell and how high up the smoke kids do it stick their hands right in you gotta keep them away or they'll do it like bugs who get too close and burn up I see why they try once why they want to touch I can see it in Eddie's eyes in the white man's eyes that stare at the flame they want to touch to put them in and see if it keeps hurting I can understand why kids do it cause I want to touch myself just like one I want to put my hand in I want to go to smoke and see how high . . .